NOT USED TO

Cute

BECCA SEYMOUR

RAINBOW TREE PUBLISHING

ALSO BY BECCA SEYMOUR

Coming Home Collection

Realigned

Amalgamated

True-Blue Series

Let Me Show You (#1)

I've Got You (#2)

Becoming Us (#3)

Thinking It Over (#4)

Always For You (#4.5)

It's Not You (#5)

Urban Fantasy Romance

Thicker Than Water

Stand-Alone Contemporary

Not Used To Cute

For information, contact the author:
authorbeccaseymour@gmail.com

Editing: Hot Tree Editing

Cover Designer: BookSmith Design

Publisher: Rainbow Tree Publishing

E-book: ISBN: 978-1-922359-39-1

paperback: ISBN: 978-1-922359-40-7

Charlene.
Love Junior Burger x

ONE

ELIJAH

THE ANIMATED man before me barely took a breath. I was as amused as I was terrified that he'd pass out any minute.

But hell, he was cute.

I wasn't used to cute.

In recent years, I was used to loose and easy. Not the best qualities to attach myself to, but still, the combination kept me occupied. Though I was the first to admit my satisfaction tended to last the length of time it took them to give me head, or for me to pound into a faceless man. Sebastian was none of these things. And the ringer was, that freaked me the hell out as much as it turned me on.

When he'd trailed in behind my sister, Harriet, and her husband, Drake, along with Drake's crazy-arse family, I took notice. It wasn't unusual for me to take a dip and sample whatever was on offer. It came with the territory of owning a bar, but a reaction to cute was something different altogether.

"So what do you do when you're not working?"

I pulled my gaze from admiring his lips and the subtle curve of his mouth. The curve turned into sweet smiles when he spoke, which pulled the happiness to his eyes. Who knew that was even possible?

"I just shoot the shit." I took a gulp of beer, realizing one, how pathetic that sounded, and two, that I did jack shit in my free time.

It was easy to blame my need to look after my younger sister, Harriet—I'd been all she'd had for a long time—but it was no longer an excuse I could use, not with Drake in her life. It had since become my own laziness along with having no desire to put up with the drama and demands a relationship usually meant. I needed both as much as I needed a hole in the head. I had enough bull dealing with keeping Bar QK running and successful. Running a gay bar in a city would be hard, but here in a small coastal town in the Sunshine Coast meant I had to be on my game.

"Alrighty, jack shit sounds…." He hesitated, searching for the right word.

"Lame," I answered as he said, "Fun."

Sebastian's laughter burst free, loud and strangely sweet. Enough for me to raise my brows and offer him a quick smile.

"What about you?" I asked, and then took another pull of beer, finishing off the bottle.

I thought he'd been animated before, but hell, his eyes lit up and his lips lifted as he spoke, his hands gesturing wildly as his voice took on a hypnotic tone. "Well, there's so much I love doing. I love surfing. Do you surf?" He didn't give me time to respond. "I don't go out as often as I like"—a small frown marred his forehead for a moment before he seemed to shake it off—"but it's something I love to do. I tried sculpting recently, but it seems I'm not very artistic. I joined the local arts group too and was in a musical about six months ago. They did only cast me as the pixie though. I didn't have much to say and was only in the chorus—"

Barely stopping to breathe, he smiled and continued talking while my mind settled on one image.

Pixie.

Yes. He was like a cute little pixie. Only about five six, slim, short hair, but not buzzed, sexy little button nose. I could see him now rocking a hot pixie costume. Though, I had no idea of what that would entail. The movie with the elf, the funny one with that guy who was Santa's son or something, popped into my head. That was an elf though, right? I really should make more time for movie watching.

"—bowls club, but I think the regulars struggled a bit with me. No idea why." He shrugged.

I quirked my lips at that one, imagining Seb—which suited him more than Sebastian—joining in with the no-doubt boring-as-all-hell retirees with his perfect kind of crazy.

"And what about work?" I asked, wanting to keep him talking.

He scrunched up his nose and twisted his lips before he spoke. "Actually, I'm just looking for a new job." He sighed, his brows dipping. It was a look I didn't like on him. "The woman I replaced when temping just returned to work last week. I've been looking for something else, but the agency doesn't have anything at the moment, so on Monday I'll be doing a trek handing out my résumé, and I'll see if something comes up." His eyes connected with mine, and his mouth lifted in another smile. "It's all good though. Something always turns up. I tend to land on my feet pretty quickly."

My brain started working overtime, wanting

nothing more than to help the man before me. He was so fucking sweet, and hell, so vibrant that I had to stop from reaching out to keep him secure on his stool. "So what do you do?"

"Admin, waiting tables. Heck, I've done so much. I sometimes struggle to find something to stick to, you know? I love the work and work my arse off, but I've always gone for temp jobs. The places I've been employed have been great, but none have really fit. I always go in wondering if the rightness will be there and then a permanent opportunity will open up, but when the contract's over, to be honest, I've always been happy to move on."

Thinking hard, I glanced around my bar. We didn't need another server, else I'd have no hesitation in offering him something. I didn't even pause to consider what that meant or how messed up that was. My bar staff was family. We were tight-knit. It was rare we let anyone in the fold—the latest being Tom, who seemed like a good kid—but the man before me had all my caution melting away.

I started speaking before I'd even formed a complete thought. "I could do with someone in the office." I shrugged, aiming for nonchalance as his eyes connected with mine, his bright, open, and honest. "Carla's been begging me for ages to take on someone else in the office to help her. It would only be part-time, but if you're interested, it's yours."

A smile stretched his mouth wide. "Seriously? That would be amazing, Elijah." He stood and threw his arms around me without preamble.

I steadied myself on impact and laughed, patting his back. It was awkward. Hell, we were in the middle of the bar surrounded by my family, celebrating my sister's birthday. I'd wanted to hug the hell out of Seb and breathe him in. Instead, after a couple of awkward pats on his back, I said, "Yeah, sure. No worries at all. You can start on Monday. Come in, and Carla will talk you through everything."

I didn't own a general run-of-the-mill bar, hence the need for support in the admin department. My place also held drag shows. While not every night, we were busy and popular enough, and ensured the shows were professional enough to warrant a whole host of support.

Seb stepped away and sat back down, still smiling widely. "This is incredible. Thank you." He chewed on his bottom lip and looked away briefly before returning his gaze back to me. "And listen, how about a trial or something? You don't know me from

Adam, so this way, if things don't work out, no hard feelings. Sound good?"

Who the hell was this guy? Sweet and confident, sexy as hell with his tight jeans that hugged his arse so perfectly, plus despite his somewhat flamboyant ways, he had the smarts too. My grin was genuine as I tried to show my increased respect for him and his words. "Sounds good to me."

He lifted his bottle of beer up to me. I grabbed a new bottle that Lenny had set down for me and lifted it to his. "Congratulations." I winked before taking a deep pull, hoping my ill-thought-out job offer wouldn't bite me in the arse.

***

HARRIET INTERRUPTED US CLOSE TO MIDNIGHT, saying she was exhausted so she was leaving. I looked into her smiling eyes, a pang of pride hitting me. She'd come so far since her PTSD diagnosis, which had formed into an anxiety disorder. Hell, just eighteen months ago, leaving the bar by herself would have been impossible, let alone touching and interacting with people.

"Come on, Sebastian, we're your ride," Harriet called to him. I had barely spoken two words to my sister all night, too absorbed in the man beside me, but Harriet was in good hands and had brought a small group of friends over tonight to celebrate. I knew enough to understand they were good people.

Seb's smile was wide. "I'm ready." He turned his gaze back to me. "Thank you so much, Elijah. Seriously. I promise I won't let you down." He reached out his hand for me to shake and I took it, wishing instead for another of those hugs he'd given me earlier.

I grinned at him, happy we were in the darkened bar as I was sure heat crept across my cheeks, desire to get to know this man riding me hard. "Anytime." I focused on Harriet, who stood wide-eyed and amused as she glanced at us. Clearing my throat, I indicated my sister needed to get her butt over to me with a head lift. I pulled Harriet close. She immediately wrapped her arms around me. "Don't be a stranger, okay?"

"Okay," she answered. "Something I should know about?" she asked when she pulled away. She wouldn't have been the only one in the bar who noticed I'd been tied up in Seb the whole evening.

I narrowed my eyes at her, trying to tell myself it was no big deal, offering Seb a job. I was having a hard time convincing myself of that, so there was no way I'd be sharing any of it with Harriet. She knew me far too well. "Nope. Just get home safe and tell Drake to not keep you locked away so much."

Harriet laughed. "Righto, I'll get right on that." Before she turned, Drake appeared at her side. I took his hand in mine and stood.

After a short pat on the back, we separated. "Thanks for sorting everything for tonight," he said.

"Anytime. You know I'll do whatever makes her happy."

He nodded. "Appreciate it. I was thinking more of me dragging along my brother and brother-in-law and their friends." He grinned as he spoke, his tone lifting into a small question of sorts. Someone else who'd noticed my whole focus had been on Seb.

I peered around him, seeing Seb now stood with two couples. Damn, I'd been introduced to them but had pretty much forgotten they were here. "No worries." I chose not to bite on how I'd hogged one of the friends the whole night. "Chat soon, yeah?"

"Yeah." He took Harriet's hand, and they headed towards the waiting group. I followed their movement, my eyes landing on Seb. Our eyes connected, and that sweet grin appeared on his face again. He lifted his hand and gave me a small wave. I offered a chin lift but couldn't have kept the smirk off my face if I tried. Just as they left, the door swinging shut behind them, I jumped as a heavy hand landed on my back.

"You okay there?" My friend Cole moved past me and sat on the stool Seb had occupied all night. "Been a bit distracted?" He quirked a brow and looked far too satisfied, wearing a shit-eating grin.

I picked up the fresh beer that had appeared on the bar top at some point and took a deep pull.

"Like that, huh?"

I sighed, not wanting to answer him or get into anything Seb related. "Like what?" I did know, however, that Cole was a shit stirrer who'd go on all night if I didn't answer him. He was the only one brave and stupid enough to push me. He claimed best friend privileges, while I'd always argued he was just a cocky bear who had no boundaries.

"The cute little button you've been panting over all night, he got your panties in a twist?"

"Screw off," I growled.

He laughed loudly. "Shit, he really has. Why'd you let him leave?" He bounced his eyebrows up and down, looking like a cockhead.

"Hardly gonna force him to stay." I sighed. "Plus, I may have offered him a job." Cole's laughter became louder. "He starts in the office on Monday," I clarified. Cole was howling by the time I finished. "What? It's not that funny."

With his arms folded over his chest, Cole shook his head. "Elijah, my man, let's face it. You're screwed. After a couple of hours, you don't even touch the man, yet you offered him a job where you'll be seeing him what, a couple or so days a week? That's so much more than you wanting to have your wicked way." The arsehole was right. Bloody hell. "I can't help but see a similarity to Drake and Harriet." He grinned, looking proud of himself, as though he'd just solved some deep mystery of the world.

I stared hard at him, realising exactly what he meant. I'd hooked Harriet up with a job working for Drake's security firm, as the office manager of all things. Months later, they'd become a couple and had since married. I had to wonder if that was what my subconscious had been telling me when I'd offered Seb the position, but there was a huge part of me that had no desire to bring a guy into the fold. With business being too busy for me to have down-time beyond sleeping, my time was scarce.

But still, I'd already invited him in by offering him a job. Hell, Cole was right.

I was so screwed.

TWO

SEB

I STARED hard at my reflection, willing my eyes to brighten and my smile to ease into a more natural state, but it was no use. I sighed, and despite the frustration bubbling in my chest, my grimace-smile eased a little. Things had gone so well the past week. Elijah had been true to his word and unbelievably kind and generous. Honestly, I was still pinching myself.

Even Carla, who had been tasked to settle me in and make sure I didn't screw up too badly, had been the perfect level of calm I'd needed to not fret and do some irrevocable damage like burn the office down or triple order beer or order the wrong item that cost a stupid amount of money.

It had all been smooth sailing. Well, if I ignored the coffee incident when I'd dropped a whole trayful of steaming hot mugs on the floor before the bar opened, but since no one had been hurt, I thought I could count it as a win. Plus there was the whole printer thing. Carla had reassured me it was normal for all the lights to flash and for it to churn out countless pages of paper, though apparently, the high-pitched beeps that refused to stop until she had yanked the plug out were different. But still, I'd survived my first week relatively unscathed.

Refocusing my gaze, I thought my eyes appeared a little brighter. I struggled at times to fit in, not only in a new place at work, but it seemed life in general. I was often "too much" for many people, but everyone at the bar had been great. A few of the bar staff had flirted, which was sweet, until Elijah intervened and told them to back off and get on with work. I hadn't minded either: the flirting or the protection. Both had made me feel good and had sent tingling goodness all the way to my toes.

Just after one week, I realised that working in a place liberally painted in rainbows screamed safety and acceptance. For the first time in a long time, I didn't feel the need to tone myself down or act a particular way in my clumsy attempt at trying to fit in.

At Bar QK, I could be me.

I sighed again, this time lighter and freer. I didn't cope well when I got in a funk, and Friday night home alone didn't help much. I'd jumped in the shower after my work week, having happily waved goodbye to my new colleagues. I'd kept my ear open when I'd left just in case I overheard the mention of a group drink or a get-together, but there'd been nothing. So instead, I'd made my way back to my small apartment and tried not to think of anything beyond my great week.

Admittedly, it had taken me the time to get home to realise that it was Friday night, which was one of the busiest nights at the bar. It meant almost everyone was working. I'd almost done myself injury with how far I'd rolled my eyes back in my head. Plus there was the whole "I could have simply stuck around and sat at the bar with a beer" thing. The knowledge had pissed me off. Completely with myself, of course.

I cast my gaze away from the mirror and finished towelling off. Once dry, I reluctantly left the room to enter the rest of my empty apartment. After throwing on my jocks, I put in a load of washing and then eyed the fridge. Despite willing food to appear, or edible items beyond tomato sauce, mustard, and jam, none did. I blew out a breath. There was no way I was heading to the supermarket. I contemplated a takeaway and considered my funds.

Elijah had paid me, so I had a bit of money, though I wasn't quite sure if it was enough to splurge on takeout. Shutting the fridge door, I glanced around the space, spotting an unfinished bottle of red wine. It was rare to leave a bottle unfinished, alien even, but I'd treated myself to a bargain cleanskin on Monday and had apparently only had a couple of glasses before abandoning it.

After pouring myself a glass, I happily gulped down the contents. I had no idea what type of red wine it was, courtesy of the nature of the five-dollar bottle, but I was relieved it was a half-decent one. Ten seconds later and a glass of wine down, I made up my mind. Sod it. I could treat myself.

With practically a skip in my step as I headed to my room, determined to keep the happy buzz warming me from my good week and the wine, I threw on a pair of boardies and a singlet. I headed out of the apartment and made the short walk into town.

One of the reasons why I chose the location was

because of the easy walking distance; the other being I'd managed to get a half-decent rental deal from a friend of a friend. I liked the area. Yeah, it was a little touristy, so you never quite knew who would be milling around, but there were plenty of stores around, and many knew me as a local, which I enjoyed. Plus, it was fairly LGBTIQ friendly, which made the noisy plumbing and tiny bedroom worth it.

As I edged closer into town, I mulled over my options. Noodles were by far the cheapest option, plus Xiu Mei, who worked there, was always chatty. I walked past The Tavern, Rangoli's, and my local grocers, throwing a cheery smile at a few passers-by, but no one I knew. Sliding open the glass door of Wok Me, I immediately spotted Xiu Mei. "Hey," I called out in greeting as I made my way to the counter.

"Hey, Seb. How're things?" She threw me a smile with her greeting as she continued to prep orders.

"Really great, thanks. I've just finished my first week at my new job."

She passed an order to her dad before returning to me. "That's awesome. Where you working?"

"Over in Marcoola, at one of the bars there."

She tilted her head. "Which one?"

"Bar QK," I answered. "But I'm not bartending. Admin."

Xiu Mei bagged an order before calling out, "Forty-two?" A young couple made their way over, collected their food, and said thanks before leaving. "Really?" she then said, her excitement taking me by surprise. Wide-eyed, she looked at me as though impressed. A weird wriggling of her eyebrows up and down followed. "A bar filled with hotties, right?"

A snort freed itself from my bemused face, which was never pretty, but if she only knew just how hot some of the staff were, let alone the patrons—and that was just during the day. "Possibly. No idea what that"—I gestured to her brows—"is for though."

She leaned closer, no doubt so her dad and the family waiting for their order couldn't hear. "Well, there's been a few regulars who come here for noodles every now and then, and I have to say, Seb, holy shit. There are a few in particular that are so damn hot I have to go and stand in our huge fridge for ten minutes after they leave." She shook her head, grinning. "Lord knows what Dad thinks."

I snorted, imagining what Mr Chen would have to say about his daughter fantasising over regulars at the bar. "Hold on, how do you know they go to QK?" I asked, bemused. While Bar QK was a gay bar and hosted drag shows, which I'd yet to see, it wasn't like regulars wore a badge or anything.

"Staff with branded logos on their shirts for a start, and haven't you seen the merchandise?"

Puzzled, I shook my head. *Merchandise?*

"How do you not know this? It's got the reputation for the best gay bar—" Her face twisted in thought. "Actually, it might be the only gay bar I know of this side of Brisbane."

"It really is great."

She grinned at me. "Look at you, being all loyal and adorable."

"I am not adorable," I responded indignantly, not even bothering to straighten up so I appeared taller. My height had been the bane of my existence growing up. Now, not so much. I owned my height. Didn't mean the ridiculous digs occasionally sent my way didn't sometimes get to me. It was one of the reasons why I'd never been in Bar QK until that night with Harriet.

She'd been surprised when I told her I was a QK virgin. But when I explained to her humans in general could be arseholes, not just the straight ones, and one too many times I'd been harassed in a gay bar, she'd been sweetly indignant on my behalf. She also, much to my horror, had told me it was her big brother's bar and she'd put him straight—so to speak —and make sure all arseholes were banned. She was lovely, if not a tad naïve. "It could be my new boss who you're swooning over."

Xiu Mei's mouth gaped. "Is he that hot?" she whisper-hissed.

"I never said—"

"You mentioned swooning."

I pressed my lips together so as not to laugh loudly and draw Mr Chen's attention to us.

"So, really, is he hot? Your boss?"

I considered the question. While I already knew the answer was a hell yes, I took the time to visualise Elijah—hardly a hardship. Smirking when I thought about his toned body, his deep-brown eyes, and his stubbled jaw, I nodded. "He really is."

"Okay, Seb, seriously, next time you have a night out there, take me with you."

That time I snickered. I could imagine Xiu going to town in a place like bar QK. She'd be in her element. She'd already told me one too many times there was safety in swooning over gay guys. I sort of got her weirdness. It was one of the reasons I liked her.

Mr Chen coughed, and Xiu Mei attempted to

look like she was busy and actually did collect my order. She handed it to her dad.

Xiu Mei was the last person I would expect to want to come out drinking though. She'd always been friendly, and we'd even caught up over a couple of coffees when we'd run into each other in town, but her dad was super strict. She was still at uni and lived at home, partly so she could still help her parents and her big sister run the noodle bar. I'd invited her out a couple of times for a surf after she'd said she'd wanted to learn, but she'd always said no.

Once in front of me, she looked at me expectantly. "Erm, sure," I said, "if you can make it. I don't think it's going to be a regular thing or anything though. I've only been there once for a night out because a couple of friends dragged me along with them." It was true. My friend Sid had called me up begging me to come, saying he needed a hand in controlling his friend Matty while celebrating Harriet's birthday. And I'd understood why. While I didn't know Matty all that well, I knew he had a habit of speaking his mind. That had been obvious immediately when we'd entered the bar and he'd started interviewing the bartender about how to star in his very own drag show. He proceeded to discuss the benefits of wearing women's undies—much to his boyfriend's and Sid's amusement.

Matty's brother-in-law, Drake, though, had been horrified, while a stunned Elijah had looked mildly amused after controlling his facial expressions. His eyes had held warmth when he'd looked at our small group as we'd entered into his domain.

It was that warmth heating his stunning eyes that had immediately drawn me to him. I'd then ended up spending virtually the whole night chatting to him. By the end of it, not only had I got a new job and a crush, but it was the first night in so long that my fears and dreary memories had abated. I realised that Elijah had brought out the best in me, beckoned out the old me, the one who was carefree and relaxed and could chat for Queensland.

What was more, I liked that feeling so damn much—the old me pushing to the surface. I hated the thought of letting it go.

"Well, when it happens, please, please, please let me know." I refocused on Xiu Mei. Her eyes were lit with excitement, innocence radiating from her.

God, was I ever that young? That hopeful?

"Sure thing." And I would make an effort—well, if I ever got the courage to take a night out, and once I was sure that the regulars who attended the bar were as cool as I hoped they were.

After paying for my order and finally collecting it, I waved my goodbye, calling out thanks to Mr Chen. He nodded in my direction, offering me a small smile. There was not a chance in hell he'd be letting Xiu Mei head out for a night at a gay bar with me.

THREE

ELIJAH

FOR THE PAST MONTH, I'd been going out of my mind. My dick was constantly hard, I was getting pissy with my staff, and wherever I turned, I saw Seb, or at least remnants of him. What didn't help was that I was dealing with a couple of incidents involving hateful graffiti—once on the bar door, the other on the side wall of the building. To say I was livid was an understatement. It had also finally made me pull my finger out and get a security camera at the front of the building.

And I wasn't the only business impacted. In our small community, there were a few LGBTQ+ establishments around that had been hit. There had been nothing too serious. Though every slur had my nerve endings firing. The police had been informed and had taken a bunch of statements. But as yet, nothing had become of it.

Complacency was dangerous. I'd let my guard down after having a couple incident-free years. And while I suspected it was shithead kids simply stirring things up, the reality was this bar was my livelihood, as well as the six full-time and eight part-time staff who relied on their jobs.

If our punters felt at risk and vulnerable, then we'd be screwed. It wasn't like we were raking it in. After wages and overheads, I had enough to save a little, but not enough to take me on a round-the-world trip or anything.

I'd already wasted hours reporting the slurs to the police and scrubbing paint. And while I'd have liked to brush off the minor incidents, every alarm bell I had was ringing to the point my head was killing. Considering my unease, it wasn't that much of a shock when my concerns came to fruition. It just so happened to be Seb who bore the brunt of it.

He stood before me, splattered in red paint, his hands shaking, and a tight smile plastered to his face. From what I knew about Seb, it was anger causing the tremble through him. "Honestly, I'm fine." The ring of the office phone had his head spinning in that direction.

"Take a seat."

"I'm covered in paint."

"Sit."

His head snapped in my direction. Seb lifted his brows in surprise, and my dick took note that there was more than that one emotion playing on his face. Incredulous. Yeah, that was the word for it.

"Am I a dog?" There was no laughter or amusement in his tone or the stare he directed my way. But my demand had stopped the shaking hands, so there was that.

"Please," I offered with a smirk. "Carla will get it."

He sighed, but it sounded defeated. It wasn't a reaction I liked on him. While I'd tried my hardest to keep my distance from Seb over the past month, whenever he was here, we spent time with each other in some form or other. I knew full well my version of "trying my hardest" was bull. My blue balls meant I was usually the one to seek him out.

I'd started craving time with him. Not only was he stunning, in that fierce, cute way of his, but he was also brilliantly quirky, and hilarious to boot. He wasn't always aware when he was being funny, but it was that part of him that was so effortless that had me sniffing around him as often as possible.

What was worse, it seemed everyone who

worked at the bar, Carla included, knew it. Seb was the only one who appeared clueless of the effect he had on me. I shook my head as I stared down at him, struggling to understand the pull and not quite sure if I wanted to risk the chase or not.

Seb cradled a mug of tea. Carla had brought it over to him to try to ease his shaking hands and bring colour back into his cheeks. When he'd returned from the post office empty-handed, pale, and covered in a fair amount of paint, I'd dropped everything. Literally dropped a crate on the ground as I'd stalked towards him.

"Feeling more together?" I watched Seb carefully. While I didn't know all his tells, I was becoming good at reading his eyes and smile.

Seb released a breath and looked down at his half-empty mug. "Sort of." The words sounded reluctant. But I was impressed with his honesty.

"I'm trying really hard here, but I've gotta know what happened exactly." Despite my tight jaw and gritted teeth, my voice was deceptively calm. Seb had yet to tell us anything that had happened. I only knew something had gone down because of the obvious. The bright red paint staining his clothes, the drops on his skin, were impossible to ignore.

As he nodded, his eyes found mine. Relief settled

in my chest when strength stared back at me. Damn, he was gorgeous. "I heard the car pull over right beside me, so I looked in that direction. He started by just saying hello. I just assumed he was asking for directions or something." I bobbed my head in understanding, urging him to continue. "He seemed friendly. Just a kid really. Can't have been older than twenty-one, asked if the bar was any good, if I worked here." He paused and blew out an unsteady breath. "I didn't think anything about it until he asked if I was a girl and liked to take it."

Heat punched into my chest. I froze, willing myself to calm down and not lose my shit. "What sort of car was he driving?"

Rather than answer, Seb continued as if I hadn't spoken. "A girl." He scrunched his nose and shook his head. "What, just because I'm not seven fucking foot tall and don't have a beard? I swear, I am so over little homop—"

"Seb, baby, please focus."

His mouth dropped to an O, and a light blush covered his cheeks. The first I'd spotted on him since we'd met. "Yeah, sorry, okay, a white Holden. An older model. It was beat up and—" Seb cut himself off and went wide-eyed before saying distractedly, "The mess. It'll need clearing up and—"

"It's okay. Go on," I said, internally cringing at my slip-up.

He bobbed his head, fierce resolve in his eyes, his muscles bunching under his tee the more worked up he was getting. "Okay, well, I don't know. His friend, who I hadn't really noticed before, said something, and they started laughing. He angled his body away from the window and I assumed he was about to pull away so I turned my back anyway to get the hell away—" He cleared his throat before continuing, "— but then he called out, and then I saw the red just coming at me. It took me a moment to realise what it was. I had a serious *Carrie* moment." The pink in his cheeks turned a bright red at this point. The anger reassured me. It was a damn sight better than him being frightened.

"Shit," he continued, "I'm sorry. I dropped the package. I'll go back—"

"Jesus, Seb. It's fine." He blanched at my hard voice. I needed to get my head straight, but it was so difficult knowing Seb had been in that situation. Yet unbelievably, he was still worried about everyone else, which was something I'd quickly discovered about the man before me. He was selfless and kind. "It's no big deal," I clarified. "Lenny will head out and look, but if it's gone, it really is no big deal, okay?"

He twisted his mouth, uncertainty etched on his face.

"Hey." I reached out and palmed his cheek, brushing his cheekbone softly with the pad of my thumb. "All I meant was nothing in that parcel is more important than you, okay?" I lifted my brows and waited for an acknowledgment, so very aware this was the first time I'd touched him like this. He nodded. "We all care about you and hate you were in that situation."

Focusing on Seb's wide, bright eyes, I asked, "And what happened after that? He say anything else?"

"He told me I should consider getting therapy. That was before he snorted at himself like a dickhead, then drove off." Not once did Seb's tone dip, his voice break, or did he lose eye contact as he recounted what happened. His strength echoed in every syllable and every slow, even breath. I, however, wanted to rip the guys' goddamn heads off —whoever they might be. "I didn't get the registration." He shrugged.

"Hey, that's okay." Whoever the dung heaps were, they'd not only attacked Seb, but had known or assumed he worked here. Immediately my thoughts went to the graffiti that had appeared in the last couple of weeks around not only my place but a few of the other businesses too. It didn't take much to figure out it was likely they were connected. But if Seb was right thinking at least one of the guys was maybe twenty-one, and not the young teenagers I'd expected, that took the threat to a new level.

The thud of my heart pounded in my ears as I tried to process everything I'd heard, everything I felt, and exactly why these guys had started to be arseholes now. This was the bloody Sunny Coast, a place with sunshine and rainbows. I sighed at that. There were still a lot of bigoted wankers around too.

It was too hard to concentrate, to think rationally when all I could see was red-hot rage. It took me a second to register the touch on my arm, and another for me to pull my gaze from the floor and look at the pale hand dotted in red before following the arm, which led me to meeting Seb's clear eyes.

A lopsided grin appeared on his face, and his tentative touch became firm. I moved my arm and repositioned it so I held his hand in mine. His hand was surprisingly rough, speaking of hard work and stories untold. It was also delicate in my larger grasp. Still, he watched me, his gaze unwavering.

"You need to stop looking at me like that." I was deadly serious. With heat pulsing through my veins and the urgent desire to do damage, I was terrified about where else my erratic emotions could lead me.

His smile remained, but his eyes widened in confusion, and he dipped his head in question, leaning forwards a fraction. "Like what?" His voice lowered to a whisper.

"Like if I kissed you right now, there's no way in hell anyone's stopping us from happening." While not a whisper, my voice was rough and low.

A startled O parted his lips as his gaze danced between my eyes and my mouth. It was a reaction I enjoyed getting from him. Seb opened his mouth to speak—

"Elijah, you need me to call the police?" Cole's voice jerked Seb's head back and had him slamming his mouth shut.

I gritted my teeth, though I didn't waver from eye contact with Seb. "Just Drake for now. Also see if someone is around to take Seb to Drake's brother's." I couldn't remember for the life of me the guy's name—Drake's brother—but I knew he was friends with Seb. And right now, I didn't want him to be alone.

"On it." Cole's footsteps moved away before I heard his voice drift over as he made his calls. I was relieved as hell he was here. He ran the security firm he co-owned with my brother-in-law.

"Is that okay?" I belatedly asked. By nature I was a take charge sort of guy, and this incident made my protective streak sit up and take notice.

"Is what okay?"

"There's nowhere for you to wash up here, and I'd prefer you not to head home by yourself right now."

"Don't I need to make a statement or something?"

"That's why I'm calling Drake. He owes me one." Having a brother-in-law who was a cop came in handy every now and then. He'd tell me the best way to handle this and call it in, make the necessary statements. "I'll tell him what's going on, then we can come by for the official stuff when you're cleaned up. That okay?"

Relief shone in his eyes. "That would be amazing, thank you."

I smiled, pleased he didn't feel the need to fight me on this. "What's Drake's brother's name, and his partner?"

"Liam and Matty. I'm not good friends with them though," he quickly added.

I didn't have time to be interested, but there was

no way I couldn't be. I was desperate for any insight into Seb I could get. "No?"

"I'm Sid's friend more than anything, and through default, Ella, his fiancée, who's Matty's best friend, who's also Sid's brother." The hell with all the names! There was no way I could keep up with that tangled mess. "Sid really helped me out a while back. He was there for me, and we used to—" His eyes went wide. There went my rage again. "You okay?"

I ground my teeth so hard, the noise was obvious in the small office space. "You and Sid—" I couldn't even say it, ask it.

"Oh." He looked genuinely surprised that my pissed-off reaction was a result of his words. "Well, sort of, but not really. We had a slight thing, but more than anything he was a good friend when I needed him. He helped me get over some shit, and then he met Ella, and they were both great, but then we sort of grew apart. Plus, he was always a little more into women. You know how it is when a couple just conn—"

"Seb."

"Yeah?"

Okay, I had no idea what I wanted to say. I just knew I didn't want to hear anything about Sid, even if he was happily loved up or whatever. And sending him to Drake's where this guy could turn up…. I mentally shook myself. "Change of plan. You okay to sit tight at my sister's until I can catch up with you? She only lives a couple of roads away." I preferred this plan already. Harriet would be there, as it was her day off. It also meant Seb would be safe and available for when he needed to make a statement.

"Umm, okay." He bit his bottom lip a moment before asking, "Do you think she'll mind if I use her shower? I need clothes."

"Yep. And I'll grab you a work tee from the back. There's bound to be some boardies or something in my office too. Best ask Harriet to take a couple of photos of you first and bag the clothes, just in case."

He nodded in understanding but still asked, "So wouldn't it be best for me to just head home? It seems like a bit of a ball ache to go there rather than straight home."

I sighed but kept my eyes firmly open, really wanting to shut the conversation down and scrub my hands over my face to wipe away the stress of the last thirty minutes. I also wished like hell the installation of the staff shower I'd had approved was finalised. "I know you want to clean up, but I don't want you to be alone right now. I don't think anything else is going to happen."

He nodded. "Anyone who does that shit, throws paint and drives off, is a coward."

I agreed completely. "I also think these guys are the ones who've been targeting the bar. It's been a while since we've had to deal with such hatred." I paused a moment, meaning my next words with everything I had. "Shit, I'm sorry, Seb. You came here to work, not to be dragged into this bullshit." The next words pained me, but they needed to be said. "I understand if you le—"

"No." He shook his head slowly, a small smile on his lips. "It's okay. It's done. I hate that anyone has to deal with hateful shit as the norm. Maybe one day it'll stop happening." He sounded almost whimsical, but I recognised the desperate need to hold on to hope, that this world we lived in would do better, be better. "It's fine," he continued. "I'll go and sit with Harriet after grabbing a shower and wait for the cops. I'd like to get to know her better anyway. You get whatever it is you need to do sorted and then call me later or something."

I stared at the man before me for a moment, openly perusing him. "I'll come and collect you. No calls or something."

His slight smile split into a grin. "Okay. No or something."

HARRIET HAD BEEN into Elijah's bar a couple of times, so it wasn't like we were complete strangers, plus I knew her loosely via her collection of friends —it was how I'd met her in the first place. But despite my ability to chat the postie's head off, let alone a virtual stranger's, around Harriet I felt self-conscious, a rare occurrence and one that made no sense considering she was both sweet and quiet.

For the first hour of being there, I'd washed up, and tugged on the new tee and Elijah's shorts that were too big. But I'd pulled the cord as tight as possible to keep them up. I then sat by myself playing on my phone. Harriet had apologised repeatedly for not stopping straight away to sit with me. I'd brushed off her apology immediately, trying my hardest to reassure her. She had a couple of calls to make, and the last thing I wanted was to add work or stress to her day.

It gave me time to think though. That wasn't always a wise move when my nerves were still on edge. I'd told Elijah I was fine, but how could I not? When his brows had dipped low and a combination of worry and then anger had warred on his face, I was convinced he'd pop a gasket.

But hell, the rush of dread when the paint had hit me…. I shook my head, remembering. It had almost happened in slow motion, not the events themselves, but rather my reaction to it. A torrent of ice-cold fear had hit me first in the chest. My breath had been lost to me in that instant, and it had taken seconds for me to focus enough to encourage my lungs to work and inhale. When air had finally expanded my chest, the fear had travelled to my heart before sending me spinning and rushing to my head. It had bounced around my system and flooded me.

I'd heard the guy's words, watched his mouth move with his syllables, and while I understood them and felt them, it wasn't until he'd driven away and my feet pounded the pavement and then Elijah had wrapped his welcoming, warm arms around me that they'd sunk in.

My trembling hadn't taken long to stop, not in the safety his arms provided. He'd given me everything I'd needed to calm myself and collect my emotions and my thoughts. And while I'd been completely thrown by what had happened, I already knew enough about Elijah that he'd look out for me.

It wasn't long after Elijah had helped me refocus that my own anger had bubbled to the surface. Incredulous didn't even begin to cover the torrent of emotions threatening to overwhelm me. That someone thought they had the right to do that to me, to anyone…. I shook my head and had a moment to feel relieved as hell that this had happened to me and not Carla.

"Need some tablets?" Harriet's question gave me much-needed respite from my overthinking.

I lowered my hand from my temple. I hadn't even realised I'd been rubbing it. "That would be great. Thanks. Would a coffee be okay too? It just helps with my head."

"Sure." Turning around, she headed to the kitchen. As I watched her go, I couldn't help but think how different she was to Elijah, physically at least. Though they did share the same lovely shade of brown eyes, and despite Elijah giving off a "don't mess with me" vibe, his gaze would often land on me and the harshness would disappear and his eyes would soften, appearing almost kind, if that was even a thing. It was funny, because Harriet had the same sweet look.

I hadn't spent enough time with Harriet to know what she was like. She'd always been friendly, which I appreciated. But then, I didn't know Elijah all that well either. Well, not outside of work. We'd spoken a fair amount the few shifts a week I was at the bar. Other than Carla, I spoke to him more than anyone else, plus he always took the time to ask me about my day, my plans, my life. He was a good boss, a good guy, and hell if my heart didn't beat erratically whenever he came close or offered me a private smile. In one of my many daydreams about him, I'd decided that was exactly what they were, private. A little offering of Elijah just for me.

Returning with the coffee, Harriet handed me mine.

I relaxed a little and inhaled the delicious scent. Offering her a tentative smile, I said, "Thanks for the coffee and for letting me hang out."

With her mug in hand, Harriet sat on the over-sized chair opposite from the large sofa I sat on. "It's all good. I needed a break anyway."

"Have you been here long?"

After taking a tentative sip of her steaming drink, she answered, "Almost a couple of years now. I used to live with my brother before moving in with Drake."

"I imagine that was fun." The one thing I was aware of about Elijah and his sister was that he was super protective. "You used to work at the bar as well, right?"

"Yeah, it was good for me, but it was finally time to make a change and take a risk, you know? I can't complain. It's how Drake and I finally hooked up." I knew they were married but beyond that nothing more about Harriet or her life.

I frowned, saying, "Drake's a police officer, right? How'd you work for him?"

She smiled. "He's more of a silent partner in a security firm. But he's able to do some work for his company, mainly during vacation time. He told me it was a pain to get approval from the Queensland Police for this second job, but he obviously managed it."

"Oh, okay. Like security as in bodyguard stuff?" I had a serious hard-on for that Scottish guy in the British drama *Bodyguard*. I could respect a man in a sexy suit being all hardcore. "Must be interesting working for a security place."

Harriet laughed. "Yeah, something like that. There's a whole heap of jobs they take on. I like it most days. I struggle with new places, meeting new people, so I'm more than settled here. I work from home, having calls directed to me here, and spend a couple of days in the main office. Plus, there's no chance Drake would let me go." I raised my brows, and she laughed harder. "No, not like that. It's not like he's holding me hostage or anything. We just work well together, keep each other centred. If there comes a time in the future, and I'm talking way in the distant future, where I felt like I needed something different, he'd support me."

Smiling at Harriet, I couldn't help but wonder what it would be like to have that. I thought I'd had something similar once, but that turned to shit far too quickly. But Harriet, she was virtually bursting with happiness. I took that as a good sign, as hope that maybe I would be able to find something like she had with Drake.

While I wasn't desperate for a relationship, and in truth, falling in love terrified the pants off me, I was lonely. I also knew that loneliness was not the best of reasons to chase a relationship. It didn't mean I couldn't hope for it though… deep, deep down.

"Don't get me wrong, he'd struggle like hell with

it," she continued with a smile, "but he'd deal, eventually. He just likes to know I'm safe." She took another sip. "How about you? You seem to be getting on okay at my brother's place. I think you need a damn medal putting up with his miserable arse—"

"Oh no. He's never miserable. He's great and helpful… and kind." Flashes of Elijah and the many simple acts of kindness drifted through me with ease, bringing a smile to my face. I could happily distract myself with thoughts of Elijah. Harriet looked on with wide-eyed disbelief, amusement playing on her lips. "Seriously, he is," I continued. "He can get a bit a-holish with some of the guys, but usually when they're being all flirty and stuff. There's a couple of flirty ones who like winding me up. Not that I don't mind the attention every now and again. But he soon tells them to get back to work. He's never grumpy with me though. He even bought me a cinnamon roll last week, as I was having a bad day and almost set fire to the photocopier. It was fine though. It didn't actually set alight—"

Harriet drawing her lips into her mouth and pressing them together made me stop. I was rambling. Again. I knew I did it, a lot. Heck, all the damn time. I also knew I could frustrate and annoy people. My stomach sank. What if Harriet just wanted me to shut up and stay quiet so she could go back to work? Shit. I cleared my throat and straightened. I really wanted to get the hell out of here and home. This was getting ridiculous. I was a grown-arse man and could be trusted to be home and contact the police myself. I frowned, wondering why I'd so readily let Elijah take the lead.

I hated feeling like this, vulnerable and uncertain. It was a new development, well, sort of, and one I definitely hated. I wanted nothing more than for the Seb of the past to come back, one where I was half oblivious, half "couldn't give a damn" about people's reaction to me. It had only previously bothered me in my early teens, but I'd outgrown it quite quickly and found my footing in the world and confidence in myself.

My mum always said I was away with the fairies, and I loved that. But a couple of years ago, the Seb I liked the most, the part of me that coped and happily danced along to my own beat, had started to disappear. Even more so after the clusterfuck with my ex. I firmed my jaw, determined not to think about him, about the humiliation, or the possibility of Harriet wanting to ship me out or gag me.

"Hey, what just happened?" Harriet's voice was gentle, her tone soothing.

She was sweet, but I didn't need handling with kid gloves. Though wherever I went, people took in my size, my large blue eyes, and immediately came up with their conclusions about me. I focussed on her, biting my tongue as she had been nothing but wonderful. Pretty brown eyes greeted me, though they were framed by a frown and had dimmed with worry.

She remained silent, watching me, waiting for me to speak. Her kind eyes eased some of my gnawing frustration, though it still festered, waiting to crawl out.

"Sorry. I just really need to get out of here." I gave a self-deprecating laugh and added, "I do have a tendency not to know when to shut the hell up." Deflection was always something I excelled at.

"At no point did I consider throwing this picture frame at you to get you to be quiet." A small smile touched her lips as she indicated the wedding photograph on the table. "Yeah, you spoke a little fast, and I was worried you'd pass out from not taking a breath"—she tilted her head to the side, her smile still in place—"but I was listening to every word you said and was enjoying what I heard. Surprised, but happy."

Her comment was enough to settle me back on the sofa a little. "Surprised?" I grabbed on to the distraction.

Before answering, Harriet took another sip and then placed her coffee on the small table next to her chair. She pulled her feet up and tucked them under her. It seemed she was getting herself comfortable. Maybe I wouldn't be racing home after all.

"Oh yes. Surprised as shit. It appears my brother has the hots for you something fierce, and you, Seb, seem to want him just as bad."

My body jerked, literally and embarrassingly jerked at her words, spilling my coffee in the process. The tension was back, as was a manic pounding of my heart. On top of that, I had hot coffee seeping through my tee, burning my skin.

Harriet sprang out her seat, quickly grabbing my half-empty mug while I tugged my top away from my skin. Shit, it still burned. "Oh shit!" It was no use. I had to get the damn thing off. I yanked it over my head, and my skin cooled for a second before the heat returned. I glanced down at the large red patch on my right pec. It was so damn sore.

"Bugger. Hold on. Let me get a cold cloth." I

glanced up and watched Harriet speed out of the room while I lowered my head and attempted to blow on my burn. Mid-blow, my head snapped up at the sound of the front door opening and booted footsteps. Elijah stood wide-eyed and staring at my chest. Like a deer in headlights, I remained still, trapped in the intensity of his gaze.

Still frozen, I watched as Elijah entered the room fully. His eyes slid up my body and then fixed on mine. His gaze didn't waver as he moved closer. His wide-eyed look had since transformed into something different, something more. While the intensity remained, appreciation was evident as his eyes hooded, their focus entirely on me. I gulped, briefly wondering how events could spiral so quickly.

"Here you go." Harriet's voice startled me. "Oh, Elijah, you're here." With a dripping cloth in her hand, she'd stopped not far from the door she'd exited from. She scrutinised the two of us, a smile on her lips. Seeming to remember herself, she then rushed forward, handing me the soaked cloth. In the few moments when Elijah and I had… connected— maybe?—the soreness of my burn had disappeared. With my heart no longer pounding quite so hard at Elijah's roaming eyes, the pain reminded me it was there.

"Thanks." I gripped the cold cloth and held it to me. I winced and was sure I groaned.

Elijah stepped forward, only stopping when he was directly in front of me. "What happened? You okay?"

I had no choice but to look at him. Embarrassment, heat, and desire be damned. They had to take a back seat as my eyes fixed on his. The concern in his tone matched that on his face. "Yes," I managed to say, struggling to know how to react to his concern. "I'm okay."

Harriet took that moment to intervene. "Honestly, he's fine. Just let the cold water do its job."

I threw her a grateful look as my grip on the cloth to my chest loosened once more from when it had slackened off under Elijah's scrutiny. I inhaled from the contact of the cold water, annoyed that I should have been better prepared. My reaction once again caused Elijah to respond. This time he reached out to me, pulling my hand gently away from my chest. My breath caught in my throat, but for a whole different reason.

"Shit, we need to get you to the hospital." His gaze flicked from my chest to my face, his brows furrowed and eyes searching mine.

"Bloody hell, Elijah. Overprotective much? And I

thought you were a nightmare with me." Harriet angled her head to get a better look at my chest. Wrinkling her nose, she said, "Honestly, it looks sore as hell, but it seems more of a scald than a burn. It'll be tender for a while, but he'll be fine." She cleared her throat, drawing my attention away from her brother and over to her.

I arched my brow at her, wondering why she felt the need to reassure Elijah rather than me. Glancing at me, she smirked. "Sorry, obviously, you may want to see your GP or something, but it doesn't scream urgent, you know?"

I smiled, mildly amused at the turn of events, but still, I was sure it appeared as an embarrassed grimace.

The wet cloth being removed from my hands brought my attention to Elijah. He didn't look happy. In fact, he looked pissed off. But when he removed the cloth and placed it carefully against my chest, a new tenderness filled his eyes. They were locked on mine when he asked, "You didn't tell me what happened."

That I hadn't, nor did I plan to tell him the discussion that had led to my mishap. "Err." I shifted uncomfortably. "I was a klutz and spilt my coffee, that's all."

His eyes tightened as they zeroed in on me. "That's all?"

"Yep," I answered far too quickly.

He nodded, not appearing convinced, but it seemed as if he would give me a pass on this one. "Okay, well, are you ready to head home?"

I nodded. "Sure. There's a bus stop just down the road from the bar. If you can drop me there, I can get going." After my bizarre day, I just wanted to head home, have another shower and a nap. I assumed Elijah would tell me what was going on with the police and a statement, and while I was curious, I was too tired to ask questions.

"I'll drop you home." His voice was low and reeked of determination and no argument.

I stared him in the eyes as his almost begged me to challenge him. Instead, I released a tired breath and simply answered, "Okay. Thanks." I pulled my tee back on.

He then turned to Harriet. "You got a lid here?"

I watched Harriet smirk before heading out of the room once again. A moment later, she appeared with a helmet and a leather jacket. "These are Drake's. He won't mind."

Taking them off her, Elijah turned to me. "Here. Put these on."

My stomach dipped, and I swear to God my knees actually wobbled. "Huh?" It wasn't my most articulate of answers, but my brain-to-mouth function was struggling to keep up.

Elijah unceremoniously placed and secured the helmet on my head while I stood there dumbstruck. He then indicated for me to place my arms in the jacket, which he held out for me. I did so dutifully before standing before him as he did up my zip. Apparently, I'd lost my ability to dress myself. No way would I usually allow anyone to get away with manhandling me in such a way, but my brain was still swirling with the fact that I had a helmet on my damn head. "So, does this mean I'm going on your bike?"

His lips twitched, which, while glorious, didn't ease the pounding of my heart. He wriggled the helmet around on my head a moment, then seemingly satisfied, he dropped his hands. "Problem?"

I risked a glance at Harriet, who had since sat down but was looking at us as though we were offering her free entertainment.

"Seb."

My head whipped back to Elijah. My heart did a little flippety-flop, reacting to the sound of my name from his lips. It was deep, yet smooth like delicious chocolate. Refocusing my gaze on the man before me, I had a hard time concentrating on anything.

"Seb?" There went his delectable tone again as he rasped my name.

I shook my head, which caused Elijah to raise his brow. He looked concerned. Heck, it was a wonder he was willing to risk me going on his bike when I clearly couldn't keep a straight thought or remain focussed. Even more than that, I knew how much his bike meant to him. It was black and shiny. Admittedly, that was as much as I knew. While I knew my cars, my knowledge of bikes was unimpressive.

A few guys who worked for Elijah also had motorbikes and had tried several times to give me a crash course as they introduced me to the world of speed and engines with a collection of magazines they kept around. My glazed expression had them soon backtracking, realising it was a lost cause. Now a surfboard, I'd be all over that shit.

"Huh?" Nope. There was still no chance of being mistaken for someone eloquent. Not with my stellar dialogue, anyhow.

"You been on a motorbike before?" he pressed.

I gave a half shrug and nibbled on my bottom lip as I tried to concentrate on his question and giving him a proper answer. It was so bloody hard. Him being so close and repeating my name was distracting. His gaze dropped to my lips before I released the tender skin and answered, "I can ride a push bike." I paused and watched an almost comical eye-popping reaction from Elijah. I also heard a snicker from his sister.

A thought popped into my overstrained head. "Oh, yes. I went on a dirt bike when I was a kid. I forgot how to brake though and rode right into a fence." I lifted my arm, turned it so my elbow was raised, and eyed it. "Ran into barbed wire. That's how I got this scar." I shrugged one arm out of the jacket and glanced at it, then at Elijah. He eyed my arm warily before a hint of a smile appeared on his lips. My heart thrummed at the movement, and I continued to speak. "It really hurt. I needed six stitches. I went on a moped once too. It was fun." I scrunched my nose.

"What happened?" Elijah asked, amused.

"Well, I kinda freaked a little and grabbed on to Darren, one of my cousins, a little too hard. I think I scared him. I may have screamed a little as well. Anyway, he ended up, I don't know, mounting a kerb. It flipped us both off. I was lucky though, but Darren didn't really think so."

He coughed lightly, and I was sure he was hiding a laugh. "Why's that?"

I liked the sound that lifted his voice. I took a brief second to look at him. His eyes seemed brighter, less strained, and I was sure it was because of the generous smile that curved his lips. "Well, I kinda forgot to let go of Darren, so when we flipped, and I mean"—I spun my hands in the air, brushing against his chest briefly as I did so—"we really flipped. I landed on him. The doctor said that his injuries, rather than gravel rash or anything, were more than likely caused by me holding so tightly on to him and landing on him so hard." At this, Elijah's gaze roamed my body.

He quirked a brow. "I can't imagine you landing that hard." My eyes widened at the heat in his eyes. "You're so small. There's nothing to you."

My heart sank at his words. And never one to hide my feelings or my expressions well, I knew my face mirrored my plummeting emotions. It was crazy, I knew. But the constant focus on my size, usually accompanied by comments intended to get under my skin, got me riled up. This wasn't little man syndrome level stuff either. I wasn't the five-foot-six guy who went around saying I'd bash everyone in, but I admittedly had a complex after years of bullying. It wasn't something I was proud of, but it simply was.

It also made it hard to feel masculine when those around me treated me as something less, or something breakable. Insignificant. My cheeks heated as I gulped back my emotions. I willed my hands not to clench.

Controlling my breath after a painful gulp, I forced a smile, my eyes finally refocusing on Elijah. His features softened; his smiling face gone. Concern instead rested there, as well as a tight jaw that ticked.

"Harriet." His voice made me tense. "Head to the kitchen a minute, yeah?" As much as I wanted to pull my eyes away from the rigid Elijah in front of me, question his request, I couldn't. I stood frozen, though was aware of Harriet leaving us from the soft padding of her feet and the opening and closing of a door. "Seb." The pitch of my name from his lips was low, but this time the word was accompanied by his hand cupping my cheek. "Breathe."

Heck, that was a great idea. I should really do that. I parted my lips and inhaled deeply. The rush of air flowed through my lungs but did nothing for the erratic pounding of my heart. His hand on my face, touching my skin, the slightest of caresses was quickly spiralling to be too much. Breathe. I really did suck at the most basic of things.

"What happened?"

His words registered though made no sense.

"Just," he clarified, "everything was fine. You smiled, then it all changed. I lost it."

"Lost it?" I was convinced I'd been dropped into a conversation midpoint as I floundered to catch up. Elijah was direct, as I was, or usually was. I liked that about him. A lot. But he also had a habit of using clipped questions, or short sentences that took me a while to work out what he meant.

"I lost your smile."

"Oh." Oh! What the heck was a guy to say to that? Yeah, he'd asked a question that he wanted answered, but hot damn, that he'd lost my smile? I really hoped to God that that meant what I thought it meant. But far out, I wasn't sure my heart could handle a man like Elijah.

From the moment we'd met at his bar, there'd been a connection. It was undeniable, but still, at work he kept his distance. Admittedly, he took time out to make sure I was coping and settling in okay, but he was the boss. And he occasionally brought me treats. And maybe we chatted about a few things other than work sometimes. It was his job. Right?

Right? Okay, so perhaps he didn't quite keep his distance at work.

And then when I'd told him about what had happened with the paint, he'd seemed to have lost his guard for a few seconds and had mentioned an "us." At the time, a flurry of activity had burst free in my gut, pretty similar to the havoc currently taking place there. The thought that it was more, the possibility that he could actually *like* me like me and that Harriet was right.... Then there was the mention of that kiss, which I was sure had happened and hadn't been a figment of my imagination brought on by shock.

Heat crept through my body. I had no idea where it travelled from or was heading to, but my senses flared to life. The subtle shift of his fingers as they still made contact with my cheek, the fresh masculine scent of his aftershave hovering between the two of us, the controlled sound of his breathing, which actually deepened a little... all caught up with me and, honest to God, weakened my knees.

I wobbled a little, and he reached out his other hand, not realising I'd been leaning into him. He placed his hand on my hip to steady me.

Not quite flush with him, it didn't seem to matter as his body heat pushed against me. Warmth that was welcome and comforting pulled me in and made unbidden words spill forth. "You like my smile?" When his lips moved and it looked like he was about to speak, my filter vanished, was whisked away into the abyss and I was powerless to stop it.

"So does this mean you like me"—*please stop* —"because if you do, which is great, but are you sure? It's just that you said I was, well you know, small and stuff, and I don't know, everyone at work says you're into big guys, or at least bigger than me." *Please, make it stop.* I didn't listen to myself, despite my last comment causing his brows to lift. "You just don't seem like the kind of guy that would go for someone like me. It's just, I'm not saying I've been bashed with the ugly stick or anything"—a nervous, awful laugh escaped my lips, carrying my words—"I know some people think I'm good-looking. Not that I'm vain or anything. Nothing like that. But I saw some of the men at the bar who I know you've hooked up with, and they're nothing like me. They have a good few inches on me—in height," I quickly added. "I'm packing, and"—*for the love of all that is holy, make it stop.* I prayed for a hole, a tsunami, a vortex—"anyway, I just, well, I like it when you smile, too." I finally ran out of steam with no clue what I was talking about or even if I had a point or answered his damn question.

I dug down for my self-control and willed myself to keep my lips firmly sealed. I knew I'd farted words at him. And somehow, miraculously, he was still before me, still with his hand on my hip, yet his expression I couldn't quite figure out.

I was tempted to reach out and smooth the two lines between his brows. I'd put them there, that was a given, but despite the lines, he didn't exactly wear a frown. Nor was he smiling.

The seconds ticked by, and my ability to remain quiet became increasingly difficult. I hated silence at the best of times, but awkward silence was a killer. I opened my mouth, willpower blown, when his hand on my cheek shifted and his thumb covered my lips.

My breath hitched at the contact, my pulse picking up when his gaze wandered my face, spending a fraction longer on my lips before returning to my eyes. There was a moment, a blissful, perfect moment when I thought he would kiss me. I read it in the intensity of his stare, felt it in the air crackling between us. His words, though, had me swallowing my emotions and wanting to crawl into myself and hide. My mouth and I always got us in trouble, and if not in trouble, overlooked or pushed aside.

"Cole's still outside." His voice, while low and gravelly, held an edge and distance that wasn't there earlier. He pulled his hands away and stepped back, leaving behind a cool, unwelcome chasm. "I'll get him to take you home."

I stared back at him, the ice of rejection hitting me hard. But there went my fake smile again. "Okay. Thanks for everything." The words tasted bitter. In my own bumbling way, I'd thought I'd put myself out there. Admittedly it was a mess of words. He was allowed to say no, even without those actual words. Didn't mean I didn't feel sucker punched as he turned and headed to the door, I assumed to speak to Cole, who I hadn't even realised was here.

FIVE

ELIJAH

"WHAT ON EARTH DID YOU DO?" Harriet's tone didn't match the incredulity of her words. She was disappointed, and fuck… sad.

I wiped my palm over my face. "Drake will be here in five, then I'm heading out." I turned to look at my sister. I'd expected her to be standing with hands on hips, a fierce look of contempt and disapproval prominent. I was wrong. Tears were in her eyes, and I had no idea why. "What's wrong?"

She shook her head, and while her head dipped slightly, her eyes kept flicking to mine.

"Seriously? What's wrong?" I asked. For many years I'd been my sister's only protector, her only family, and while she now had Drake, all it took was a small hint of her being in distress and I was ready to solve all of her problems. She'd been through so much that it was impossible to change my ways. Truth be told, I never would.

"You."

"Me what?"

"Why'd you do that?"

Seb.

I closed my eyes and released a heavy breath. Looking back at Harriet, I said, "Do what?" I knew she'd call bullshit, but I did not want to talk about Seb, about what the hell was going on in my head about the man who'd entered my life like a tornado. The last thing I wanted to do was talk to my baby sister about it.

Instead of biting, she brushed away a stray tear, which made my stomach sink even further. I was having a hard enough time handling pushing Seb away, palming him off to Cole. It had taken all my willpower to watch him drive off with him. Harriet getting pissed at me was welcome. It would help me focus on a solid emotion rather than attempting to navigate through the minefield of shit pulsing through my head.

I sighed in defeat. So much for me not talking about it. I would have scoffed if I could handle the additional energy needed to react. "You know why."

Once again, she shook her head. "No." Her voice was vehement. "You always used me as an excuse; my past, my issues, my condition. I always knew that was bullshit but didn't call you out on it, and I'm sorry. I should have. I was too caught up in my own crap."

"Like hell you were. You had every right to retreat the way you did. Don't you dare say you're sorry to me for anything." My tone held no room for argument.

Her eyes softened a little. "But still, you used your need to look after me as your reason to not get close to anyone. You can't do that anymore. I'm getting there, am so much better, and I have Drake."

I lifted my shoulder in a light shrug, having no words to respond. I didn't know what she wanted or expected me to say.

"Elijah." She stepped forward. "Why did you push him away?"

I stared at my sister. My mouth clamped shut while my heart pounded in my chest. I'd been legit terrified of Seb, my reaction and draw to him. That was my truth, and there was no way anyone else would ever know that. I didn't even truly understand it myself.

When he'd rambled on, my need to kiss him had been fierce.

Shit, even back at the bar I'd admitted I wanted to kiss him. What the hell had I been thinking, saying that to him, especially after he'd just been attacked.

But through the sometimes nonsense of his words, it was so easy to see his strength as well as his insecurities. They lay out in the open for me to see. It had hit me, when my thumb had grazed his lips, that I had the power to destroy every element of good he had inside him. Seb was all light. A bright-ness lit in him when he lost himself in his words, sharing his wandering thoughts. It would be too easy to douse that. No way would I allow that to happen.

Harriet looked at me, her stare hard. I knew she didn't understand what was going on in my head or the decisions I made. She thought I pushed people away. She'd told me several times. But that wasn't technically true. I had my friends, my bar, and her. I didn't know if there was room for anyone else.

"Listen—"

Drake entering stopped me from continuing, and I couldn't have been more grateful. He glanced at the two of us, zeroing in on the upset on Harriet's face, and stiffened. "We good here?" Eyes on Harriet, he waited for her to respond before moving.

She nodded. Drake entered fully, threw me daggers, and headed over to my sister, sweeping her into his arms and then pressing a kiss on the top of her head. I watched as she leaned into him, and I wanted nothing more than to look away, but instead, I stood transfixed, taking in what they had. Their start hadn't been easy, but they were strong, and I was happy for them. My gut churned as I tried to make sense of that happiness.

I liked that she was happy, was relieved that Drake kept her safe.

"Right. I'm gone." I spun and pulled open the door.

"Elijah." Harriet's unsteady voice stopped me. "Love you. Stay safe."

Throwing her a wink, I answered, "Always. You too." I sent Drake a chin lift, then headed out and mounted my bike. Revving my engine, I peeled out of the parking lot and headed to the bar. Cole had said he'd head back there after, and I needed to sort out a way to make sure my bar and staff were safe. My thoughts immediately travelled to Seb and his crestfallen face.

I'd hurt him, but better hurting him now, setting

the lines, than me letting him down like I had every other relationship I had ever had.

"Tʰᴀᴛ won't work." I shook my head at Cole.

He cracked his neck from side to side, rubbing his hand over his dark buzzcut hair. It was so unlike my dishevelled hair that I tended to hide away under beanies and caps. I watched as his jaw tightened before he lifted his brows at me. "Right. So what do you suggest then?"

I was being difficult, and I knew it. "Nothing," I sighed. "Ignore me. I'm being a prick."

He grunted, amusement in his raised brows. "You think?"

I squinted at him and gave a noncommittal shrug. "Whatever."

This time, Cole snorted. "Listen, I know as much as you do that this is all screwed, but what else is going on?"

Deliberately keeping my shoulders relaxed, I asked, "What're you talking about?"

After a few beats of silence, I looked his way and then sighed when he stared at me, unflinching, with a hard gaze. Rubbing my palm over my face, I considered my response. There was no way I would be sharing with him or anyone how tied up in knots I was over Seb. Clenching my jaw, deciding stubbornness was the safest option, I opened my mouth to fob him off but was interrupted by Cole's phone ringing.

I grinned, picked up my beer, and took a swig.

His hard stare remained fixed on me a moment longer before he reached for his phone and answered. "Yo?"

I looked around the bar as he spoke. There were only a few guys around, and Lenny serving at the bar. I held up my almost empty bottle when I caught his eyes, and he nodded, throwing me a small smile. Lenny was a good guy. As Banjo's brother, a guy who'd I'd grown up measuring dicks alongside, he'd transitioned into his position at Bar QK with ease over the past few months. It was a sort of given that I'd give him a chance, since I'd known him for most of my life.

I'd seen him sparingly over the years. And I'd told Banjo on more than one occasion that I thought his ex was a douche. His smile had rarely lit his eyes, something that hadn't sat comfortably with his brother or me.

He'd only been working the bar for us for the

past six months, and that was because finally, after a couple of years of being involved with a controlling shithead, he'd managed to break free of him. Since leaving school, he had barely done anything but work or stay at home, courtesy of his jealous ex who expected him to be at his beck and call unless he was bringing in the cash. I knew Banjo was angry that his brother had played the happy, dutiful boyfriend for so long, livid with himself that despite the many challenges and questions he'd thrown his younger brother's way over the years, Lenny had never disclosed just how bad his relationship had become.

I was relieved his ex was out of the picture. At twenty-five, Lenny was too young to be so downtrodden and wary. I snorted as he set my beer in front of me, the irony of my words and my own situation not lost on me.

"What?" Lenny asked, his brow cocked high.

I shook my head. "Nothing, Len, really."

He leaned his elbows on the bar and gave me a look of disbelief. I grinned, remembering him as a young kid. Hell, from about four, he'd followed me and Banjo around, always in the way, always sweet as hell. We'd started high school not long after he was born, and while Banjo and I had somehow gotten roped into babysitting more often than we'd like, both of us protected him fiercely.

Despite his youth, 'cause he seemed a damn sight younger than me, there was a hardness in his eyes. It kinda made him wise beyond his years.

"If this is about a certain new member of staff who has a penchant for talking too much and leaving a trail of destruction in his wake, I think you should stop worrying and go for it."

My brows sprang high, making Lenny laugh. "Am I that obvious?"

He seemed to take pity on me as he pulled in his amusement. "To me and perhaps a few others who've known you forever."

I sighed at that.

"Seb is a really good guy. What's the problem?"

My shrug was lame. I knew it, but it was all I could offer.

Lenny pursed his lips a little, a crease bunching between his brows. "Listen, I've got my own set of theories about why you hold yourself back and make yourself unattainable."

"You do?" I shook my head. "Actually, I don't think I want to know."

"But how about I tell you anyway?" A mischievous smile lifted his lips.

"Or I could just walk away?" I countered.

"Then I could follow you. There's a few tables I can clear along the way."

"Or," I sassed, "I could just fire your arse."

"Ha! As if. You need me too much, not only because I'm a genius behind the bar and manage to make tips in a country that doesn't tip—" He paused, and I couldn't help but agree with how right he was. He did have a fan club who visited every weekend just to watch him make cocktails. There were plenty of regulars and newbies alike that wanted a shot at him. "—but also, you know I'm the only one who will say it as it is and put you straight."

I quirked my brow at his wording, and he rolled his eyes at me.

"Get me a shot, and I'll plant my arse here and listen, I suppose."

"Good choice," he said, turning and making a beeline for the back wall lined with liquor.

"Actually, best make it a double."

Who knew, maybe he could help me pull my head out my backside and figure out how to get over my fear of letting Seb in? Because that look Seb had shot my way when I'd sent him home without me wasn't something I thought I could handle again.

SIX

SEB

THE COWARD in me had me calling in sick the next day. I couldn't afford it, but my humiliation was too raw. I spent the day eating own-brand ice cream, a whole litre to myself. I also managed to score a four-dollar cleanskin bottle of wine too, saving a whole dollar on a dodgy special that was running.

The combination wasn't the greatest, but it was needed for me to get over myself.

Past relationships of mine had a way of ending epically badly. And while Elijah and I didn't have a relationship at all, I'd let my fanciful mind think that he cared for me beyond that of employer looking out for his employee. I'd allowed myself to believe that just because my attraction was fierce and thoughts of him overwhelmed me, he must have surely felt the same way. And then there was that kiss declaration.

But how wrong I was.

My alarm blared. I cut it off and exhaled. There was no choice but to get my arse out of bed and into work. It was drawing to the end of the month, which meant the bills had started to arrive thick and fast.

But I could do this.

I could play the game, fix a smile on my face, and carry on and earn some cash. What would also help was I could get a surf in. It had been a couple of weeks since I'd last hit the waves—a long time for me. Heading out with my board would help clear my head and get things into perspective. Really, I should have got up at the ass crack of dawn to go, but after the ice cream and cheap booze yesterday, there was no way that would have happened.

After sorting myself out, I headed out, making the bus just in time. The bus meant I was twenty minutes early, but much better that than me being late, so I took a breath and entered the bar. It was already open, as it catered for breakfast, making the most of the tourist trade. I waved at Lenny, who was at the coffee machine. His smile was wide as he greeted me. My shoulders relaxed a fraction, grateful that Bar QK was so welcoming. Despite my embarrassment about seeing Elijah, it was the friendly faces of Lenny and then Carla that reaffirmed sticking this job out was the right thing to do. I'd get over my fanciful crush.

"Feeling better, honey?" Carla asked, heading over and wrapping me up in her arms.

Warmth rushed through me at this woman's kindness. "I really am, thanks," I said, pulling away.

"We've all been so worried." She looped her arm through mine and led me to my small desk, settled me in, and then poured me a glass of water.

"You have?"

"Of course, what with the paint and what you went through." She shook her head and tutted.

"Oh yeah." I cringed internally. Was it bad that I'd all but forgotten about the weird paint incident? While it had shaken me at the time, every thought and emotion since had been overrun with Elijah. The day of the incident, I'd ended up making a police statement to Drake when he'd shown up at my small flat a couple hours after I'd arrived home. But other than that, I didn't know what would happen or could happen.

"When you didn't come in yesterday," Carla said, her voice turning into a hushed whisper, "Elijah was a nightmare. He started demanding that I rock up at yours to make sure you were okay. I told him I texted and that you'd responded to every single one, so finally he gave in, but bloody hell, nightmare."

Confusion had me dipping my brows low. "It will have been because of the paint, is all." That was the only reason I could think of. He'd made his intentions perfectly clear when I'd been at his sister's house and he had sent me on my way.

As I spoke, Carla snorted out a laugh. "Whatever you say."

Before I had the opportunity to question her more, the phone on her desk rang, and I turned to the paperwork on mine. I knew I had a bunch of orders to make, plus I'd been tasked to coordinate an upcoming fire and evacuation plan audit.

It was early afternoon before I stood and stretched, having got on top of the most urgent tasks. But it was no good. I had to have a conversation with Elijah about the inspection. I picked up my notes and left the small back office, going in search of my boss.

"That's never going to happen."

I stumbled when I heard Elijah's harsh words and

paused just to the side of the open doorway to his office.

"But you know my mouth on your cock—"

My eyes sprang open at the voice I didn't recognise.

"I said no." Elijah cut him off.

"But it's never been a problem before. Why now?"

Elijah's sigh was loud and frustrated. "I'm not interested, so back off before you humiliate yourself even more."

Movement and chair shifting followed. A voice in my head screamed at me to leave, but I remained rooted to the spot, unable to pull myself away.

"It's that bright-eyed twink, right?" The voice was full of derision. "Everyone is talking about it, about you sniffing around him." A spiteful laugh followed. "Heard he's not interested, and frankly, I'm surprised, Elijah. I thought you liked your fucks to have a little more substance."

Nausea swirled in my gut, twirling with anger that woke inside me. While I couldn't be sure this guy was talking about me, it was too much of a coincidence for it not to be. But he had so many facts wrong. I was the one doing the silent panting, Elijah certainly wasn't interested, and bloody twink.... I balled my hands into fists. It wasn't a term I liked, wasn't a label I wanted. For those who did, good on them. I was all for people making their own choices and embracing their own identities. But that was one I didn't want.

A chair shifting caught my attention. Elijah's low voice followed, sounding more menacing than I'd ever heard before. "If you want to keep your contract with us, you'll back the fuck off, and you'll never mention Seb again. You hear me?"

My heart hammered in my chest. The sound rushed to my ears, making it hard to concentrate.

"Holy shit, it's true. You are stuck on him."

I was sure whoever this guy was had a death wish. While I'd never seen Elijah react in any way violently, between his physique, his broodiness, and his take-no-shit attitude, I had no difficulty visualising him shutting someone up with a damaging punch. The thought should have scared me. But there was one thing I was certain of about Elijah— okay, more than one thing—but when it came to violence, I imagined it would be a last resort and only in defence.

"Matthew, get the fuck out."

A high-pitched snort followed, clearly from this Matthew. "Okay, okay, no need to go all Hulk on me." He sighed almost whimsically. "I'll miss your cock in my mouth, but I will say— Now, now, nothing shitty to say, honest." I wondered what Elijah had done elicit such a reaction. Curiosity burned through me as I waited for him to continue. "He must be something really special to have caught your attention and kept it."

The chair moved again, and a huff from Elijah followed. "He is."

I couldn't think. Couldn't breathe. Standing like a statue, I was close to passing the hell out, struggling with getting air into my lungs. When I finally did, I spun around quickly, needing to get out of there.

"Hey, Seb," Carla called, "you finished with Elijah already? Is he free?"

I willed the floor beneath me to open up and swallow me whole. It didn't happen. Instead, the sound of Elijah's office door swinging open filled the space, and I felt the colour in my cheeks drain.

"Seb?" Elijah's voice had me moving.

"Uhh, quick call to make. The copier is burning. Got to go."

I just reacted, no real idea about the words I spewed. I just had to get out of there. I brushed past Carla, not quite breaking into a run, but moving as though the hounds of hell were chasing me. Reaching the rear exit, I burst through the doors and headed to the car park. There was a small wall just beyond where a few cars were parked. I reached it quickly and sat, knowing it would block me from anyone's view.

What had I been thinking? Hanging outside of Elijah's office like a creeper wasn't my smartest move. Not only would he know that, he'd also know I was a coward, as I'd run out of there quick smart.

The job had been going so well too. Perhaps it was my cue to move on and look for something else.

Sitting alone, nothing but my ragged breaths and my fast-beating heart as company, I froze when I heard the hinges of the rear exit open. While I knew I could be, should be better than this… better than hiding, I was too concerned about the consequences should it be Elijah.

Heavy-footed bootsteps made their way over the bitumen.

I closed my eyes briefly before figuring I needed to pull my head out of my arse and deal with this head-on.

Flicking my eyes open, I peered up just as Elijah stepped around the cars. His unreadable expression greeted me. When his gaze flickered over me, there was a softening there, confusing me even more.

Finding my voice, I said, "Hey." The man had

done nothing wrong. But everything about this situation screamed discomfort.

"Hey," he said back. "Mind if I join you?"

I paused at that, unsure how to answer. It seemed my mouth was doing it for me, saying, "Actually, I was thinking about heading out early, if that's okay? I promise to meet with you first thing in the morning to sort the audit particulars."

Quiet for a beat, he pressed his lips together, his head tilting a little as if trying to figure me out. I considered letting him off the hook right now by telling him a few had tried and all had failed. But my insecurities wouldn't allow it. I was like a yo-yo. I knew this. And while I wouldn't be apologising for my highs and lows on any given day, I knew I owed Elijah an apology for listening in on his conversation.

I stood to do just that, the words on my tongue when he cut me off, saying, "Where are you going?"

I winced a little guiltily but told him the truth. "I need to clear my head, so I'm going to go for a surf."

"I have boards here."

His words surprised me. "You surf?"

A wide grin stretched across his lips, and my heart ramped up. "I definitely do."

"Oh." I had no idea. I should know better than to make judgments about people.

"Rather than you head home, I can put two boards I have here in my truck, and we can go together." He'd lost his smile as he spoke, and I couldn't help but wonder if he anticipated I'd say no.

There was no chance of that.

SEVEN

ELIJAH

THE WAVES WEREN'T the greatest, but getting out into the water, especially with Seb, was worth the effort. And the smile he cast my way just before he threw himself off the board after riding it in confirmed I'd done exactly the right thing.

I followed suit, paddling out. As my fingers scooped the water, a rush of calm flowed through me. A grin spread across my face to the point I was sure I looked slightly manic, but damn, was it a rush. Freedom coursed along my limbs, elevating my soul, relaxing me in a way I hadn't felt in a long time.

A slight burn tugged at my arms. I loved this, loved the escapism the fresh air and waves offered. I inhaled deeply and feeling the tip of the wave, sprung to my feet, impressed as hell I didn't clamber or fall off immediately—unlike my previous three attempts. Angling low, I caught my balance and all but soared through the water. As I drifted along the small face of the wave, joy lit me up, settling in my bones.

My smile didn't ease, somehow getting bigger, aching at the stretch on my face. As the wave drew to an end, I gently turned on the flat, taking control of my ride in and throwing Seb a huge grin, punching my fists in the air with a loud "Hell yes!" before throwing myself off the board.

I easily broke free of the water, my head lifting to the surface. A couple of strokes later, I held onto my board and hauled my arse back on it. With my shit-eating smile intact, I followed up with a loud laugh, eyes immediately on Seb, who mirrored my delight.

I sat on my board, bobbing in the moving water, my eyes still on Seb as he joined me. "All good?" I asked when he was within hearing distance.

He nodded emphatically, his smile finally removing the worry I'd seen earlier. "Not the best, but it was good to ride in, get myself watered. You?"

I laughed, loving his enthusiasm. "Yeah, the same. Nice that I actually made that one in, though."

"Do you get out often?" he asked as he reached my side and sat up, legs wide across the board.

Momentarily distracted by his smooth skin, both sun-kissed and lickable, it took me a moment to register his words. I dragged my gaze away, my eyes connecting with his. I should have blushed, perhaps should have been sorry that it was obvious I was checking him out, but he was gorgeous. Too easily my eyes gravitated to him, and I could happily waste hours getting lost in the man. "No," I finally answered, my focus dipping to his mouth when he swept his tongue over his bottom lip, "certainly not often enough. Thanks for letting me tag along." I smiled over at him. A burst of flutters in my gut appeared when his reaction to my smile was immediate.

I wasn't a fool. I knew he was interested and was confident he'd be up for us exploring this connection between us. But that didn't mean I should simply take what was on offer. He was worth more than that.

"I'm pleased you came." His mouth quirked when he spoke. "It's rare I'm surprised by people these days, and you surfing was a pleasant one."

"Yeah?" Was it bad that I was happy I'd surprised him? Based on the lightness in his eyes focussed my way, I knew it shouldn't be bad. Making someone feel good was, well, good, right?

So why did it feel like I was setting Seb up for disappointment?

"Definitely," he said. His eyes remained on mine, his focus intent. "So I may have been avoiding you," he admitted.

Surprise at his honesty fluttered through me. "I'm sorry you felt the need to do that," I responded. It was clear I'd hurt him, and me blowing hot and cold was not helping. I huffed out a breath, considering how honest I should be. As far as I was aware, he'd been nothing but real with me, so perhaps it was about time I offered some back.

"It's okay. You were just being nice, and I think I misread the situation." Seb looked away and shrugged.

Guilt was never pleasant, and the feeling reinforced the need to set him straight. It didn't matter that I was shit scared of doing so. Putting myself out there petrified me. Finally, I swallowed my nerves and forced out, "You didn't misread anything."

Immediately, he flicked his gaze back to mine, his eyes wide.

A small huff-like laugh escaped but I continued, saying, "I was in a long-term relationship." I didn't think it was possible, but his brows sprang even higher. "We were together for years, but when my sister was going through hell, struggling with her PTSD, well, my focus turned to her and making sure she recovered." The rhythm of the waves bobbed us up and down, the movement easing the difficulty of my words. Seb's full attention remained on me as I continued, "My ex decided he couldn't handle what my sister was going through, and he suggested I look into a medical facility for her."

"Holy shit, really?" Seb's brows dipped low and distaste seemed to wash over him.

"Yeah, and when I said no and continued to care for her, bitter doesn't even describe him." I shook my head in memory. "It turned out he was offering himself up for any willing dick while badmouthing me and Harriet too. It was Cole who finally discovered what was going on and told me."

"I can't imagine how shitty that must have been for you." His gaze softened, but there was no pity in their depths.

"It was." I rubbed my hand over the back of my head and clasped my neck. "It took me a long time to deal with my anger," I admitted, "and I'll be honest, trust has been the biggest challenge."

Bobbing his head in understanding, Seb remained quiet, as if taking in all my words and letting them settle. I appreciated that he wasn't full of platitudes. "You know," he eventually said after a few moments of just the waves keeping us company, "I don't think I've ever fully trusted anyone." His words startled me.

"What do you mean?" I asked.

He shrugged. "My parents were dickheads and kicked me out when I officially came out. I was fifteen."

Sadness churned in my gut, while anger that anyone could mistreat Seb, one of the sweetest men I knew, beat against my chest.

"I managed to get through school by bouncing around friends' houses, sleeping on couches or bedroom floors. I then met someone when I started training at the local TAFE, and he screwed me over so damn fast I almost got whiplash. After that, I just started kind of expecting it from people, you know? Use and abuse… screwing me over. Taking what they want and then pissing off." A soft smile lifted his lips. "Then you gave me a chance and have never taken anything from me."

My heart lurched at his words.

"You only expected me to do my job." The sweet intensity of his gaze caught in the wind, whirring around us.

Seb was incredible. Through every word he

shared, there was not a sob story attached, no demand for pity or expectation that anyone owed him anything. There was a gentle truth instead. Acceptance. And I fucking hated that he'd ever been made to feel that being treated like shit was the norm.

I swallowed down my anger at myself, knowing I'd only perpetuated that with how I'd treated him after the attack. God, I was a wanker.

Before I could say anything, confess he had me tied up in knots, his gaze flicked out to sea. "I'm going to catch this one." All I could do was nod as I watched him paddle hard, his sinewy muscles lithe and strong. A moment later, he popped up on his board like it was an extension of him. The movement effortless, the ease obvious, and as he rode it in, he'd never looked so free or quite so magnificent.

The reality of how incredible this complicated man was punched me in the gut with the ferocity of a ten-foot wave. The question was, could I pull my head out of my arse and put my heart out there for him?

EIGHT

SEB

WHEN I WOKE to my alarm, there was no hesitation this morning as I threw back my covers, preparing to ready for work. Yesterday, the afternoon I'd spent with Elijah was quite possibly the best time I'd ever had.

We'd talked easily and freely, had laughed and joked, and more times than once, when I'd turned, his eyes had been set on me, but he hadn't pulled away.

Each time, my stomach had flipped and my heart had thudded hard. The feeling was alien, but I couldn't say I hated it.

When I'd told him a bit about my past, his anger had been palpable, and emotion had shone through his eyes with what I liked to think was respect. I'd come a long way over the years. While sadness and frustration were still familiar forces in my life, I refused to turn over and accept that was my future. I wanted to be happy, and since meeting Elijah, feeling the connection and recognising his acceptance of who I was went a long way with reminding me I was worth all the happiness.

It didn't matter if nothing happened between us —even though if that was the reality, it would suck. Instead, he, as well as the group of people who'd so readily accepted me into their fold at the bar, was the push I needed to keep my head held high and chase the joy life could give me.

Not even the shabby curtains or the chipped tiles of my small apartment could dull my outlook this morning. Because screw that. I paid for this place myself. There were no government handouts, no exchanging of favours, just me and sticking it out at work and picking up my hard-earned pay cheque.

"Morning," I greeted Carla as I stepped into the small office.

She turned her head in my direction, her grin immediate and wide. "Morning, Seb. You're looking much more yourself this morning." She surprised me by standing and wrapping me up in a warm hug. It seemed this would be how she greeted me daily. I could definitely get used to it. I embraced her back. "I was worried about you," she said, giving me an extra squeeze.

My heart filled, so grateful there were so many good people recently in my life. "Thank you. I'm great. I'm feeling much better."

She stepped away, her gaze raking over me. "Good surf yesterday?" The twinkle in her eyes had me laughing.

"It was just what I needed," I said, not offering any more.

"I just bet it was," she sassed.

My smile was wide as I got myself sorted and settled, looking at my to-do list.

"What's on the agenda today?" she asked, giving me grace and not pushing for details.

The notepad before me was fairly full, but my priority was the fire inspection. "As soon as Elijah is in, I need to go through what's needed for the audit this Sunday. I imagine that will take up all my time today, unless you need me for anything else in particular?"

She shook her head. "Nope. You're all good to

focus on that. It's a pain in the arse ensuring we're up to spec, important, but yeah…." She bit on the end of her pen. "Are you sure you're okay to be here on Sunday for it? I know it will go over your hours."

Immediately, I bobbed my head. "Absolutely. It's no problem."

Carla's lips curved. "Thank you. Plus, there's a couple of real hotties in the local department. Hopefully one of them will turn up for the inspection, so the eye candy will make it worth your while."

I laughed and looked down to switch on the PC.

She continued, "There's something about a man in uniform, right? You have a sexy firefighter fantasy?"

I laughed again, eyes fixed to the keyboard as I typed in the password. "Is that a trick question? Who doesn't?"

"Maybe after Sunday, you'll be given some fresh material to get hot and heavy over?" Humour filled her voice, while I snorted.

"I think I've got more than enough to be swooning over. Not sure I need anything more complicated than what's filling my head at the moment."

"Wise decision there."

I froze at Elijah's deep, grumbly voice. Wide-eyed, I looked up fast, gaze connecting with his. One of his brows was quirked, and his stare was intense.

"Don't be swayed by a man in uniform. Carla should know better," Elijah said, and I heard Carla snort out a laugh.

I risked a glance at her, and she simply smiled, looking thoroughly entertained. My eyes narrowed as I wondered how long Elijah had been standing there and if she'd known.

After clearing my throat, I said to Elijah, "Do you have time to talk through what's needed for Sunday, please?" Sidetracking was the only option here.

He nodded and then lifted his hands, indicating towards his right one. "I got you a coffee. We can chat in my office." The rapid beat of my heart caught my breath. He'd been out and got me a coffee. Internally, I rolled my eyes at myself. He probably got everyone one.

"Aw, you got me a coffee," Carla sassed. "You shouldn't have."

"I didn't," he said, shooting her a look.

Her laughter followed us out of the room as I grabbed my files and cradled my coffee, as though it was the best gift in the world, while willing my heart to calm the hell down. It was a coffee. It wasn't an offer of a blow job, for Christ's sake. Shaking my head at myself, pleased that Elijah was leading the way as I silently gave myself a stern talking to, I worked hard to calm down.

By the time he opened his office door and waited until I brushed on by him before closing it, I was no closer to my heart behaving. "Thanks for the coffee," I said quickly as I looked around his small space.

"I think I got it right. Vanilla cappuccino, right?"

My smile was immediate that he knew how I liked my coffee on the rare occasions I could treat myself to a takeout one. "Perfect, thank you."

We stared at each other a beat, neither moving. The man was hotness personified, and being in such a confined space with him was a little heady. Add in what I'd overheard the last time I was here….

"Shall we get started?" he finally said, and just in time too, as the walls had begun to close in on me.

"Yeah, sure." I placed the files on his desk.

For an hour we talked through the process, Elijah clarifying a few aspects that I needed to know. We then did a walk around the bar as well as the small kitchen, storerooms, and office spaces.

Almost everything appeared to be in order as far as we could tell, which was a relief.

I'd previously done my own walk around and implemented a few changes, which Elijah seemed impressed by. I'd grinned a little too widely receiving his praise.

After spending a couple of hours together, we headed back to the small office space. At the doorway, I hovered, peering over at him. Even though the past two hours were most definitely work-focussed, we'd laughed and joked, and I'd only found myself rambling a couple of times.

"Are you planning on being here tonight?" he asked me, taking me by surprise.

"Oh, no, I hadn't planned on it."

"You should. You've yet to see any of the shows, right?"

I shook my head. "Not yet, no."

The smile on his mouth came as soon as I responded. "In that case, you have to. Tonight it's Lady Bra Ga. She's one of the favourites and brings in a fun crowd."

I'd heard all about the various nights and performers Bar QK hosted and had considered coming once or twice. Without excess cash, it always made a night out tricky. Especially considering the entrance charge on such nights. But perhaps I could splash out and then simply prop up the bar. I didn't need booze to have a good time.

"Yeah," I finally said. "I'll check it out."

It would be good to do something outside of the norm and break up the monotony a little. "It starts at eight thirty, right?"

He bobbed his head as he answered, "Yeah. Speak to one of the guys out front, and they'll save a stool for you."

I smiled at that. "Thanks. Will do."

There was a moment of stillness that could have easily become awkward. Before it got so bad that I started spouting off rubbish, he saved us both. "Okay, Seb, thanks for today. I'll see you tonight." He turned after casting me a smile and walked away, leaving me wondering if he was working or socialising tonight. My stomach flipped over itself when I hoped it was the latter.

I stepped into the small back office, Carla immediately greeting me. "All okay?"

I headed to my desk and cast her a smile. "Yes. I think we're all good," I answered.

"Superb." She threw me a small wink and continued with whatever task she was working on while I sat.

It was impossible to not think about tonight,

though, or the reality of my finances. "Carla," I said as nonchalantly as possible.

"Yeah?" She glanced my way.

"I was thinking about heading in to watch the show tonight," I said.

"I think that's a brilliant idea," she said keenly. "Lady Bra Ga's shows are a blast."

I grinned. "That's what I've heard." I picked up my pen, simply for something to do as I asked, "Remind me what the door charge is?"

She tilted her head a little before she answered, "It's fifteen dollars."

I bobbed my head, throwing her a smile while figuring out how much cash I had in my wallet. I did have an emergency twenty-dollar note I kept hidden away for bills or food, but I didn't think this consti- tuted as that. But with Elijah the one to have asked me…. I sighed. I was such a sucker.

"You know," Carla said, "employees don't have to pay a cover charge to get in for the events held here."

Surprise hit me, warring with embarrassment. Was I so easy to read? "Oh, okay. Thanks for letting me know."

Her kind eyes were directed my way as she nodded. It seemed as though she wanted to say something else, as a quiet contemplation drifted over her. Not wanting to get into anything with her, as there was not a chance in hell I'd be getting personal with anyone about my finances, I quickly said, "After these few orders I have to make, I have some time. You need me on anything for you?"

She shook her head. "I'm all good, thanks."

I offered a chin lift and set about sorting my orders.

The rest of my shift flew by. With only working part-time, I was out of here by four and not due back till Tuesday. It was only the exception of me offering to come in on Sunday for the fire inspection that meant I'd be getting some extra hours in. I'd volunteered, not expecting to get paid, but Carla telling me that I would definitely be paid for the few extra hours I worked was a relief.

I had an ad-hoc job delivering store leaflets once a month for some extra cash. The extra money helped me stay afloat. It was easy work, which I didn't mind one bit. My next drop wasn't until the following Friday, and I'd have the whole weekend to deliver seven hundred leaflets.

With the few hours extra I'd be paid on Sunday, it would mean I could buy a couple of beers at least. And with Elijah being there tonight, those would be helpful to get me to relax so I wouldn't ramble and make a spectacle of myself.

Smooth was not my forte.

Once home, fed, and getting ready, I tugged on the nicest jeans I had. They were old and well-loved but fit well. They also hadn't faded too much, so the dark blue made them look decent. The one purchase I'd allowed myself over the past six weeks, a pale blue Superdry tee I'd spotted on sale, clung to my chest. The luxury of surfing being free, beyond the bars of wax I splurged on, meant I was in good shape and had strong arms. It set my guns off pretty damn well, and I allowed myself a small smile in the mirror in my room.

With the fairly regular bus service, as in one running every hour out here, I could get to the bar with ease. I'd just have to make sure I was on the five past ten bus back. It would mean an early night, but it would be worth it.

After the short journey, my stomach dipped and dived. It wasn't like it was unusual for me to be by myself, and while at least tonight I would know most of the staff, or at least recognise their faces, it didn't stop my nerves from making themselves known.

I considered all I knew about Elijah. It had been impossible to not listen to the gossip. While there'd been nothing too recent about his exploits, he had a reputation of hooking up and seemed to have a steady flow of broken hearts in his wake.

His conquests didn't bother me. We all had histories, and who didn't like getting off? But the thought that I may see him in action tonight made me queasy.

I shook the feeling aside as I made my way to the bar, relieved to see Mitchell on the door.

"Hey, Seb," he greeted, offering me a wide smile. "How are you doing tonight?"

My smile mirrored his. "Good, thanks. Excited about out the show."

He bobbed his head. "Lady Bra Ga is pretty great. Be careful though…" His brow lifted. "She has a reputation for eating pretty boys up, especially fresh faces."

I laughed, appreciating the humour in his voice. "Noted, thanks. I'll be sure to hide at the bar. Not sure I can handle a man-eater," I jested.

He chuckled as he opened the door for me. "Have a good night." A wink followed his words as I stepped into the bar.

The room was cast in dim light, the small stage to the left lit in twinkling lights. A range of bodies littered the space—small groups, a few couples, and mainly men, with what looked to be some clusters of women. A happy mumble of voices, punctuated with laughter, filtered through the space, and immediately I relaxed, loving the vibe.

I'd never not been comfortable at Bar QK, but with this busy crowd and the energy floating around the place, ease settled through me. Walking through the crowd, I returned a few smiles sent my way, not recognising anyone. I didn't know who was a regular or who was here just for the show, but the head dips and friendly faces were a welcome sight.

As I neared the bar, I angled to the right, towards the end of the bar, when I heard my name. Lenny waved, and I gladly made my way over.

"The boss man asked for me to make sure you had a stool." He dipped his head at the empty stool and threw me a wink.

"Oh, thanks." Heat touched my cheeks, as not only had I forgotten to ask for myself on my way out this afternoon, but Elijah had remembered and taken care of it for me.

"What'll it be?"

I only had just over an hour to enjoy the show before I'd have to dash out to catch the last bus, so it wasn't like I had to pace myself. I'd also figured it was cheaper to go for a spirit simply on the grounds it would make me feel buzzed. "Vodka soda, please."

Lenny bobbed his head and went to the shelf displaying the liquor. He grabbed the more expensive bottle, and I cringed. "Actually, the Trivoski will do, thanks."

He glanced over at me, hand still on the Chopin. Making his way back towards me, picking up a glass en route, he said, "Boss man's got this covered, so let's not drink the stuff that's going to destroy your head."

I froze at that, the heat already in my cheeks beginning to burn. I shook my head. "Honestly, it's fine. Even more so if he's paying for it."

Lenny's gaze flicked behind me and slightly to the right before he returned his attention to making me a drink. A moment later, warmth hit my back and I stilled, knowing the presence belonged to Elijah.

"There's no way you're drinking that shit," he said low, next to my ear. "My treat."

Angling to look at him, I was immediately ensnared in his deep gaze. I didn't even eye him up and down to see what he was wearing, too caught up in the look in his eyes.

"You sure?" I asked, not wanting to insult the guy, nor wanting to take the piss either.

"I'm positive."

I nodded, my lips curving up. "Thank you."

He took the empty stool next to me, angling a little in my direction. "Anytime. I'm just pleased you made it."

"You are?" I asked, not holding back my widening grin.

"I am. The last time we had a drink together was when we met."

I scrunched my nose at that, saying, "I remember. I kind of accosted you, huh. Chatted your head off a bit. Sorry about that."

"I'm not. I'm pleased you came that night."

Oh, how I wish I had. I snorted at the thought, the sound causing Elijah to quirk both his brow and his lips at me, and I kinda figured he knew what I was snorting at.

"Well, you did offer me a job, which I'm so grateful for. Seriously, thank you."

"You're good at organising the place. I think it was a good choice."

Warmth spread over me at his compliment. They were few and far between in my life, and getting one from Elijah was crazy dangerous for my heart.

Movement in my peripheral vision caught my attention, and my gut clenched as I recognised the hot blond who sometimes came in for lunch. One of the bar staff had told me he'd hooked up with Elijah a time or two.

The blond and I were polar opposites. He had a good five inches on me, was broad-shouldered, and while not overly muscular, he clearly took care of himself.

He stepped into our space, focus solely on Elijah. "Hey, E." The shortening of Elijah's name had me bristling at the familiarity and sent my discomfort into overdrive. "I didn't see you back here."

I pulled my eyes away from the two men, clamping down on my drink and taking a sip.

"Kirk," Elijah said, his voice polite. "You here for the show?"

"And hopefully some time with you," Kirk said, and that was my cue.

"Uhm, I'll see you later. Thanks for the drink." I downed the contents and all but threw myself off my stool. I eased through the crowd of bodies, not having realised it had filled up so quickly. But that was the thing with Elijah. He captured my attention completely. Dangerous and so not good for my heart or survival.

I shook my head as I headed towards the back room, needing fresh air but not wanting to face Mitchell or anyone else. As I opened the rear exit, the cooler air hit me. I inhaled deeply, mentally shaking myself.

Elijah had been nothing but kind and generous to me. With so little good in my life, it was no wonder I read his invitation as being something more. That was completely on me. And regardless of what I'd heard when I'd been outside of his office, I could only assume he'd said what he had to get that guy gone.

A humourless laugh escaped me. I was a dick at times. What I needed was to shake this off, remind myself that it was okay to crush on a guy from afar, and give myself a reality check about anything more happening.

Kirk had been the reminder I'd needed for that.

Tilting my head back, I couldn't see any stars, the rear entrance too enclosed for a good view, and with just a little too much light pollution. I jerked my head down when I heard movement. Eyes focussed and narrowed, I couldn't work out what was in the distance.

Only two businesses led to this rear exit, and I

couldn't imagine the neighbouring store needing to be here at this time of night.

A small light flickered. A cigarette. Sharp laughter followed hard, mumbled words. Unable to see what was going on, I angled away from the door a little. There was a streetlight at the very end of the narrow entryway, and once whoever it was walked in that direction, I'd probably see who it was.

With no idea why my curiosity was piqued, I continued to look in that direction. The sound of scuffing shoes letting me know at least one person was moving. A few moments later, I saw a man. He turned in the direction of the person he'd walked away from, saying something I couldn't hear. Though the snarl in the tone was crystal clear. And even though he was cast in shadow, I recognised his face immediately. It was the guy from the other day. The dude with the paint.

Edging back to the door, my heart beating loudly and verging on frantic, I reached out and grabbed the handle. I eased the door open and stepped back into the safety of the rear entryway. Moving out of the direct way of the door, I hovered, wondering what to do, and considered I should have perhaps hung back to see who was outside with the paint guy.

The rear door opening had me freezing and flicking my eyes in its direction.

Tom stood in the doorway, surprise registering on his face as he stepped fully inside.

"Hey, Seb. All okay back here?"

I didn't know this bartender well and had only met him a couple of times, as he tended to work night shifts after I'd left for the day. A tightness around his eyes and the smile that didn't quite sit naturally made him appear far more uncomfortable than I was.

"Yep. Just taking a breather from the crowds," I said, my lips flipping up in a practiced smile.

He nodded, something like relief passing through his eyes. "Yeah, it can get crazy on these nights." He indicated over his shoulder towards the exit. "I was just taking a breather while I can, you know?"

My smile remained the same. "Best get back to it."

"Yep." He walked past me, leaving me questioning what I should do.

That Tom had been speaking to the guy didn't look great, but it didn't mean Tom was involved necessarily. Whatever had been said outside didn't sound pleasant from the tones I'd heard. I could have easily asked Tom who the man was and what they'd been speaking about, but the possibility of stepping in the middle of something sent my gut twisting with unease. Trusting Elijah to know what was best and how to handle this, I'd pass on the info and follow his lead.

The thought sent a blast of shock through me.

I trusted Elijah, yet I'd just run away from him, my feelings far too bloody sensitive for my own good. But I supposed that was why I'd run. It was rare I let people in at all, and the few times I had and was then burnt, recovery was unsurprisingly shit.

Resolve calmed my racing heart. If Tom was involved somehow with those guys, and even worse, bringing them in to Bar QK somehow, that had to stop. Fast.

I headed back to the main bar, immediately hit by the crowd and the wall of heat and noise. Not sure where Elijah would be, I angled straight towards the oak bar, seeing Lenny. Sometimes being a little more compact had its benefits, and slipping around the bodies to make my way to Lenny was exactly that.

Hands on the wooden surface, I stood up on my tiptoes, trying to see better around the area, looking first in the direction of where I'd been sitting. Elijah wasn't there, nor was the blond. I swallowed back my reaction to the thought that they may have gone somewhere together and refocussed.

"Lenny," I called. He was just passing over three bottles of beer to a customer when his eyes landed on me. A quick lift of his head in acknowledgment, and he finished serving before heading in my direction.

"Okay, Seb?" Concern shone in his eyes. "Boss man was looking for you. He seemed worried."

I bobbed my head. "Know where he is?" As I spoke, out the corner of my eye, I saw Tom serving a customer and side-eyed him as I waited for Lenny to answer me.

"Not sure. He headed towards the front."

"Okay, thanks." If I hadn't been looking carefully, I would have missed Tom dipping his hand in his pocket before returning what I assumed was change, in the same hand he'd dipped into his pocket, to a guy at the bar. Wide-eyed, I looked on in horror. I needed to pull away before he saw me. Subtlety was never my strong suit.

"Hey, you sure you're all right?" Lenny's brows were dipped low.

"Yeah. Thanks. If you see Elijah, let him know I need to talk to him, yeah?"

He bobbed his head, already reaching towards

the fridge as a woman next to me called her order over the loud voices.

Turning, I angled in the direction of the front entrance. This was so bad. Maybe. Possibly. What had Tom passed to the guy? There was the possibility I was wrong and that Tom wasn't linked to the dick who'd attacked me, but I'd prefer to humiliate myself and be mistaken, rather than keeping my mouth shut and this impacting on Elijah's business.

NINE

ELIJAH

AS SOON AS Seb had left, I'd understood why. He'd already told me my staff gossiped, and with Kirk appearing at my side and offering himself up on a platter, it took but a second for the reason to be clear.

It both pissed me off and made my cock twinge at the same time.

I hated that Seb thought Kirk would be the focus of my attention rather than him. Truth be told, since Seb had started, I'd hadn't accepted a single blow job or quick screw. With Seb constantly on my mind, it made it impossible to want anyone else's mouth on me, and I certainly didn't want to be buried deep inside anyone but him.

Years of meaningless sex had finally run its

course, and all because of a cute guy who didn't know his own worth.

And my cock twitching? That'd be my ego recognising that Seb was jealous.

A few minutes after disentangling myself from Kirk and then getting sidetracked by the lighting guy for the show who had questions, I was able to go and look for him. I figured he'd wanted some air so headed towards the main entrance. Mitchell was at the front. He worked for Cole and my brother-in-law's security firm and was the regular here on our more popular drag nights.

He was great with the customers, took no shit, nor did he get involved in anyone's drama.

"Elijah," he greeted when I stepped outside, my gaze scanning the pavement and across the road.

"Hey, Mitchell. You know Seb, right?"

I looked in his direction and caught his smile at the mention of Seb's name, bristling a little at the interest I thought I saw there. "Yeah. He's got a hell of a lot of awkward personality, right?" His grin stretched wide. "It's sweet as hell."

My brows raised high at that. It didn't matter that he was absolutely right. Seb was a good guy and a gorgeous man. That other guys were noticing the latter didn't sit well. A flush of heat spread through me. Not exactly in anger, but since I didn't want anyone else noticing just how much of a catch Seb was, a flare of jealousy spiked in my chest, unfamiliar and uncomfortable.

"He is that," I said, trying to keep my tone neutral. "He's unavailable though, yeah?" Apparently, my aim for neutral hit the ground with a thud, my instruction sounding a lot like interest. Who was I trying to kid? I wanted Seb so damn badly, I had barely slept since he'd started. And especially after I'd been such a cockhead to him, and my sister had put me in my place, my already poor sleep was weighed down with both guilt and regret.

I should have hauled his arse on my bike, taken him home, and made sure he was okay. And at least been there when he'd given his police statement. It didn't matter that I wasn't sure if he'd ever allow me to do that, as he'd made it clear he could take care of himself. Of that I had no doubt.

But I didn't think anyone ever had looked out for him, had his back, and simply been there for him. And I hated that for him.

Lost in my own thoughts of Seb and my attraction and concern for him, it took me a moment to realise Mitchell was silently grinning like a fool. I huffed out a breath. There was no point in asking him why. He read people well and knew me well enough to know he'd never seen me claim a man before.

"Shit just got real, huh?" He nodded, approval shining in his eyes.

Ignoring him while internally agreeing, I asked, "So he's not been out here in the last five minutes or so?"

The easy-going smile disappeared off Mitchell's face. I could almost see understanding slam into him as his gaze swept the area. "No," he answered, still looking. "Should he be?"

A new tension had me stiffening as I wondered where he could have gone. There was the office, I supposed, out back, but I'd assumed this was his direction. "I just need to find him."

"Should I be worried? Need me to call Jada?"

Jada was the other security detail who worked these nights, but she remained vigilant inside, not only keeping an eye on our performers, but making sure the crowd was only here to have a good time and not start anything.

"Yeah, please," I said. "If she spots him, ask her to keep him with her. Call me if you—"

The loud music and chattering from the indoor

crowd disturbed the air as the door opened, drawing our attention to the doorway.

"Seb," I said, relief carrying his name. My tension didn't drop though. Worry creased his brow, and he was pale, not what I'd expect from someone who'd just been in a crowded bar. "What's wrong?" I asked immediately, stepping into his space and reaching out to touch his forearm.

Soft skin and peppermint overwhelmed my senses, but not enough to distract me from my concern.

"Can I speak to you?" he said. His voice was unnaturally low, controlled, and my concern grew.

"Of course. Inside?" I asked, but he was already shaking his head. Seb flicked his eyes over to Mitchell, who stood alert and a little to my right and behind me. I had no doubt so he could be ready to jump in if need be. "Okay. Here or the wall?" I indicated to the low brick wall about ten metres away.

"Wall's good."

I slipped my hand down his arm and took his hand, holding it. Before walking away, I turned my attention to Mitchell. Alert and apprehensive eyes stared back at me. I simply nodded, and received one in return. He knew I'd reach out to him should I need to.

Begrudgingly I acknowledged Mitchell liked Seb. But then, everyone did. Even those who didn't necessarily understand him well. I expected some struggled with working out the outgoing and talkative Seb compared to the clumsy and sometimes painfully shy and uncertain Seb. All I knew was that I didn't have to understand these variations of him. I simply respected each trait and appreciated each and every one for making up the man beside me. The man who made me feel that he was worth the risk.

For him, I could be brave.

But first, I needed to find out what had him spooked. The trepidation on his face didn't scream of a man jealous of an old hook-up. This was something more.

I sat, not releasing Seb's hand, and angled to look at him. Even in the darkness, only lit by the few streetlights, his handsome face was visible. While he wasn't feminine, there was a softness to him. It spoke of kindness and compassion. And amongst all of that was fierce resolve I'd only seen a time or two.

"Okay," he said, surprising me that he didn't need prompting. "I'm pretty sure I saw something out back and would never come to you about this if my spidey-senses weren't tingling"—I swallowed my smile at that, not wanting to distract him—"but they were off-the-charts tingling to the point I was considering how I could create some makeshift web." My lips twitched, but it didn't interrupt his flow as he continued. "I think Tom is doing something dodgy."

Immediately, my humour slipped away, and I tensed, completely focussed on Seb's words.

"The guy from the whole *Carrie* incident—"

"Was in the bar?

Seb shook his head. "No, he was out the back."

"As in the rear alley?" I clarified, my brain already whizzing and coming up with scenarios rather than waiting patiently for him to continue.

"Yeah. I didn't hear what was being said, but he was clearly talking to someone and not on a phone. He also sounded angry."

"Did you see who?" I asked, my brows pinching together.

"No, but as soon as I slipped back inside, Tom came in from the back entry."

Tom and the paint guy? Surprise had me leaning back. The kid hadn't worked here long, maybe three months, but his references had checked out and there'd been nothing but positive feedback about him. He kept to himself but was always friendly enough with the customers.

I also knew for a fact the guy was pan. So him being in cahoots with the paint guy and homophobic didn't sit right.

"Tom Miller?" I checked.

"Yeah, the bartender. He came in, seemed surprised to see me. When I headed back to the main bar to find you, I watched him serve someone, head to the till, then his hand went into his pocket before handing the change and maybe something else to the bloke he was serving." Seb was wide-eyed and a little breathless by the time he finished speaking. "I didn't see what he passed over, but after being sure he met with that guy, and after your suspicions about the graffiti, it just screamed dodgy. I had to tell you. I'd hate for something to happen to you or the bar."

The concern in his voice was almost enough to have me reaching out to him with more than my hand currently gripping his, but I couldn't handle the distraction, not when my mind was working over-time. I had to think how to play this. There was no real evidence, but Seb, even though I'd known him for less time than Tom, I believed and trusted. If he saw more in the situation, then I'd be chasing it up.

"Was it okay that I came to you about this?" he asked, his gaze roaming my face. "The last thing I want to do is cause issues, and honestly, I hope I'm wrong, but—"

I squeezed his hand, having forgotten for a moment I was still clasping him to me. "You did the right thing, thank you."

Relief entered his eyes as he stared back at me. "That's good," he said with a nod. He then swallowed, the sound audible in the pocket of quiet we had. "What are you going to do?"

I pulled my lips into my mouth before huffing out a breath. "I'm not sure yet. I need to figure this out. Work out the right way to handle this." The last thing I wanted was for the incidents to step up. By far the attack on Seb was the worst, but it would be so easy for the situation to spiral to something more serious, destroying my place in the process while taking down these arseholes who were stirring shit up. Cole was the obvious answer, and I needed to act fast. If Tom was connected in some way, I needed to intervene.

That also meant I needed to talk to him tonight, which would be a shitshow with how busy the bar was.

"You think you can do me a favour?"

Seb was bobbing his head before I'd finished

speaking, settling the anxiety churning my gut a fraction. "Of course, anything."

A genuine smile lifted my lips as I looked at him, not something I'd thought possible considering the situation. "Do you think you can help work the bar tonight? I'm going to pull Tom away and have a sit-down with him. As soon as I do, can you help?"

The barest of hesitations preceded his "Sure, but full disclosure, I'm not great at bar work, but I'll give it a go. Shit," he then said. Worry dipped his brows low.

"What's wrong?"

"My last bus home is soon, but it's fine, I'll—"

"Don't worry about that. I'll make sure you get home." Ideally, I'd be doing that task myself. I wanted to make amends for the other day. Plus, any chance to spend some extra time with Seb was something I could get on board with.

He eyeballed me a little, making me curious about what he was thinking. I didn't have to wait long before he said, "Are you planning to take me home, or will you be passing that chore off?"

Guilt flared to life in my chest, even more so that he wasn't being pissy. There was no snark in his tone, just what seemed like genuine curiosity. It was time to make good on my internal promises. "If you'll let me take you home, I'm more than okay with that."

Seb tilted his head to the side, his eye contact steady. "And you won't change your mind at the last second, because honestly, Elijah, I'm not sure how much more of the mixed messages I can handle." Even in the darkness, I could see the flush spread over his face. "Uhm, perhaps I shouldn't have said that. It's not fair of me to—"

"No," I said immediately. "It's okay, and it is fair. I was a jerk the other day. That was on me. Let me make it right."

The twitch of his lips sent my heart soaring, and when it turned into a full grin, it was only reality hammering away in my head that kept me from saying screw it all and taking him home right now.

"Making it right sounds good."

It would be easy to stay here like this for as long as possible, but a conversation with Tom was imminent. "Okay, if you head back to the bar and prop it up for a while longer while I take a quick look at the security cameras, I'll let you know when to take over. Is that all right?"

He nodded and stood, hand still in mine. I followed his movements and peered down at him. Bright eyes gazed up at me. It was impossible not to react to the expression on his face. Impossible not to lean down and finally capture his mouth with my own.

The touch of our lips was soft, gentle, a combination of tentative touches and smooth caresses. We brushed against each other, the rhythm natural and in synch. There were no false starts, no worry about how to move; instead, the connection was effortless.

My groan matched his at the contact, and I held him closer, unconsciously tugging him firmly into my arms. I engulfed him, his body snug and feeling so very right against mine. My tongue swept across his for the barest of moments, the touch lighting a fire in me that if I didn't stop, I'd struggle to remember my responsibilities.

After slowing the kiss, I reluctantly pulled away, breathless and wanting nothing more than to take things so much further than acceptable out on the street.

A glassy-eyed Seb stared up at me, mouth still slightly open, his gaze roaming my eyes and my lips. "So," he said, "that just happened." His mouth spread into a smile. "We can definitely end the night doing that tonight."

His words drew a laugh from me, the sound too loud in the darkness. "Good plan," I answered, finding the willpower to tug his hand and lead him back to the front door.

"Just checking," Seb said quietly, "I'm keeping all of this super quiet, right?"

"I don't care who knows we kissed." My response was quick and fierce. He chuckled. "Oh," I said, chagrined. "You mean Tom?"

He nodded, a cute smile on his lips. "Yes, but I'm happy about not hiding the kiss."

I shook off my embarrassment, allowing his words to warm me instead. "Me too," I responded, adding, "And yeah, on the keeping it quiet. Nobody's to know anything, please."

"Got it," he said. "My lips are sealed."

I smirked at the man who managed to make me feel like I was walking on air, despite the drama about to unfold. Once sure my bar was safe, I could only imagine the sparks we'd create. Without distraction, and my attention solely on Seb, the kiss we'd just shared would reach levels I was sure would change me, quite possibly forever.

TEN

AS WARNED, I was not a natural at bar work. But I tried my hardest to get orders right, and as the evening progressed and the amazing Lady Bra Ga performed a show that kept distracting me with its brilliance, the customers didn't seem to care so much.

But seriously, back to her performance. Lady Bra Ga was incredible. She'd taken on the whole Lady Gaga persona, but times that by a gazillion of awesome.

Energy thrummed around the bar, the customers responding to her energetic performance. The whole time I remained transfixed.

"Amazeballs, right?" Lenny said next to me,

drawing my attention from Lady Bra Ga's set of "Bad Romance."

"I've never seen anyone like her," I said in awe, returning my gaze to the woman on stage wowing the crowd spectacularly. Despite being out since a teenager, my situation had limited experiencing the wonders of live shows and performances to zero.

"Holy shit, you're a show virgin," Lenny said, glee evident in his voice.

I jerked my head in his direction, my brows lowering until finally his words registered. I snorted. "Yeah, suppose I am. I think I may have a new obsession."

A smile so filled with wonder and happiness crossed his face that it was impossible to not laugh.

"You okay there?" I asked.

He nodded immediately. "Yep. She just has one more song, though, so why don't you take a break to enjoy it?" He indicated towards the open bar stool.

I glanced around the bar. While the place was still full, there was a lull in the need for drinks, the audience too wrapped up in the performance. Maddie was also serving tonight, but she was handling her area well and wasn't rushed off her feet.

"You sure?" I finally asked.

"Absolutely. Here, hold on a minute." He turned around, grabbed the vodka—the good stuff from earlier—and poured me a drink. "You saved my arse today stepping in when Tom had to race off. Enjoy."

My grin stretched wide. "Thank you." I happily took the drink off him and made my way back around the bar and to the empty bar stool, my mind briefly wandering to Elijah and what was happening.

My curiosity didn't last long, my focus turning fully to the stage.

Lady Bra Ga, covered in sequins, red lace, and wearing the highest heels I'd ever seen, finished with a frozen "Vogue"-esque position before there was the briefest of movements and sparklers crackled and flared on the bra contraption she'd been wearing during the performance.

I laughed and cheered, stood and hollered right along with the rest of the crowd.

"Thank you, you beautiful souls," she said over the applause. "With just one last song, be prepared to finish… big!"

The blast of "Poker Face" came over the speakers, and the whole bar cheered. The lights of the stage dimmed before rising, and four hot-as-hell men stood there, posed and leaving very little to the imagination. Wide-eyed, I looked on, excited for the performance as I gazed around the stage, realizing Lady Bra Ga had disappeared.

I swiped my drink and took a large gulp, wincing slightly at how strong it was before setting the glass down and directing my whole focus to the stage.

The beat of the song continued, and the men started to move, the oil on their bodies glistening. A moment before the first words, she stepped onto the stage, bold and brash and looking incredible wearing black and white.

And then, she nailed it, performing with ease, stepping off the stage into the crowd of fans. A path parted for her as she made her way around while she rubbed her hand through heads of hair and stroked down chests. I grinned the whole time, the atmosphere explosive, taking large sips of my vodka, only to pause, my eyebrows springing up to my hairline when her eyes connected with mine and she strutted over, her sights apparently set.

She sang before me, her hand in my hair, and my wide smile was back, laughter flittering through my chest. Just before she reached the final chorus, she bopped my nose, threw me a wink, blew someone behind me a kiss—which I realised was Lenny when I peered over my shoulder—and strutted her long legs back to the stage.

The final chords of the song played, the spotlight focussed on her, and once more, I was out of my seat, cheering and making my voice hoarse. I then spun and looked at Lenny. "Did you do that?" I asked, and when he nodded, the kindness directed my way made me practically giddy.

It didn't matter that there were parts of this evening that were a shitshow and admittedly freaked me out a bit. I'd never been more grateful to have been dragged into this bar a few weeks ago and thrust into Elijah's world.

"Thank you so much. You're the best." Kindness had been rarely genuine or free in my past. But after meeting this bunch of good people in recent weeks, I realised decent human beings really did exist.

"Anytime, Seb. Another drink?" he asked as I placed down my empty glass.

It would be so nice to say yes. That last drink had gone down easily even though it had seemed to take a long time to drink in the ten-minute set, but with the performance over, the customers were beginning to move. I squinted a little, wondering whether I was actually moving, or perhaps the bar was. I wasn't quite sure.

"He'd love one."

The voice made my heart leap. It was the perfect

blend of low and gruff. I turned, my gaze landing on Elijah. I was able to zero in on him. And while he was a little fuzzy around the edges, his exhaustion was clear. Tiredness pinched his brows, but the smile lifting his lips seemed only for me.

"There's only fifteen minutes before we close. Have a drink. I'll jump behind the bar and then we'll look at getting you home." He stepped closer midway through his words, fully in my space to the point my head angled backward to peer up at him.

This time I had no choice but to squint, trying to get him into focus. His nearness sent a thrill through me, closely followed by desire.

"You don't need to get me drunk to get me home." The words spilled out. "Not that I'm saying that's what you're trying to do, but I'm just saying." I heard Lenny's snort behind me but decided it was better if I ignored him. Not that I wanted to look away from Elijah. With his piercing eyes and the light stubble shadowing his strong jaw, he was too pretty to not simply gaze at.

"You think I'm pretty, huh?"

I wrinkled my nose. "That was meant for my head, but yes, you are. Not sure how you manage the rugged thing you have going on while still being pretty. It's hard not to jump up right now and climb you." I closed one eye, hoping it would make me hear better, because I was sure I just said those words aloud. "It doesn't help," I mumbled to myself. Maybe if I tried the other one.

His eyes widened comically, and I grinned, liking his smile and wondering if I was the reason for it. With the eye thing going on, which I was almost sure didn't help me tune in and focus, my head remained fuzzy. But at his smile, my chest warmed and tingled.

"I've only had two drinks," I said, smiling up at him. I held up my hand and aimed to hold up two fingers. I crinkled my nose, seeing four. "Huh." I shrugged, leaning slightly.

"The equivalent of six" came from over my shoulder. This time I looked back and squinted again. Lenny stopped moving from side to side when I did so.

"Huh?" I pursed my lips and bobbed my head. "It's why I want to climb you like a tree." I also wondered how I'd managed to drink so much in such a short span of time.

Elijah's laugh was loud and seriously made me consider doing just that. I pulled my gaze away, reminding myself I was in public, but even more importantly, his bar. I let that thought hold me down and in place.

"On second thought, perhaps a water for Seb, please, Lenny." Elijah leaned down a little, moving his face closer to mine. "Why don't you sit back at the bar, drink some water, and if you get sober enough, we'll look into the tree climbing?"

I shifted quickly. "The stool moved," I said, clinging onto Elijah's arms, aware I had been close to face-planting. "Did someone move the stool?"

Soft eyes looked down at me, and Elijah helped get me settled, turned me to face the bar, and placed the water in my hands. He was looking after me. The knowledge hit me, weaving its way through my fuzzy head and double vision. When I picked up the water, I felt a touch to the top of my head. A kiss. Grin stretching wide before I took a sip, I focussed on drinking plenty and diluting the booze in my system.

Mission Sober coming right on up, I thought, gulping back the contents while already wondering if Elijah would stop for a burger on the way home.

"It won't stop." I winced. "Hush. Don't speak so loud."

A not-so-soft snort had me side-eyeing the man to my right. "Just let me know if I need to pull over," he said.

I shuddered at the thought, still drunk but sober enough to finally realise what was going on and that any sudden movements would have me hurling. My grunt was all I managed in way of answer as I leaned against the cool metal of the car door and eased the window down further. The cooler night air helped calm the swirling in my gut a fraction, but I didn't know if it would be enough.

In my defence, I'd had a hell of a week. Between the whole paint shitshow, knowledge that some dodgy dudes were responsible for it, and said dodgy dudes were possibly up to no good where I worked and that I was the tattletale, it was no wonder I'd got hammered. Even though it was Lenny who'd been topping up my drink without me realising.

"If I puke," I said, eyes closed and staying as still as possible, "make Lenny clean the car."

"Yeah, I just may do that." The sound of his shifting reached me, but I had no energy to check. "You don't have a pet or anything, right?"

My brows scrunched at the question. "No."

"Okay."

Why was on the tip of my tongue, right alongside a build-up of saliva. Instead of speaking, I swallowed, then exhaled.

"You good?"

Another grunt escaped my mouth.

A touch on my arm, along with my name spoken softly, jerked me upright. I blinked rapidly, becoming aware that we were parked, the engine was off, and that I'd clearly fallen asleep. Quickly, I touched my mouth, not quite sure if I was checking for drool or vomit. But finding neither, I was able to breathe a little steadier.

My gaze then connected with Elijah. His seat belt was off, and he was angled towards me, leaning slightly in my space. "Hey," I said, pleased that my nausea seemed to have calmed.

"Hey," he said, his mouth curving upwards. "Listen, I've brought you home, as you were never really clear about where you lived, and honestly, I wasn't sure if you'd be okay."

"Oh." I supposed I could have reminded him of my employee file, but he'd probably just assumed I could show him the way. Once that thought fizzled away, warmth slowly swept over me. Once again, he was looking out for me. "Thank you," I finally said. "That was nice of you."

A flicker of relief passed through his eyes, and he bobbed his head. "Come on. Let's get in the house, get a drink, and head to bed."

I nodded, wishing that my head was clearer to take everything about this moment and about his space in. But since I'd be staying over, there was always tomorrow. After I managed to clamber out of the car, I closed the door behind me, taking in the bare minimum to see he lived in a single-level home, and while he had neighbours, they were far enough away to signal he had a bit of land.

"Need help?" Elijah's voice made me jump in the darkness of night. Other than two small lights shining from the neighbouring properties, and the one porch light on his home, the night was ink black. It made losing myself so very easy, especially with the fuzziness still making it difficult to think straight.

"Think I'm okay. Thanks." I followed his movement, my eyes having adjusted a little, hoping a step didn't jump out at me or something. Relieved when I reached the lantern on the porch without stumbling, I did a mental fist bump and quickly checked my hands were by my sides and I actually wasn't doing it. It wouldn't have been the first time.

Elijah flicked the entrance light on, bathing the room in bright white. I winced, preferring the dark so I wouldn't have to squint so much. Focussing on putting one foot in front of the other, I followed Elijah into the kitchen, grateful when he switched on a small table lamp against the wall on a sideboard. "Water and paracetamol?" he asked.

"That would be great, thanks." I waited, feet firmly planted, remembering how to not sway. It was too late to even pretend to act sober, and while I supposed I should be embarrassed, I figured I hadn't actually done anything to humiliate myself. So I'd gotten drunk? It wasn't the worst thing in the world.

A moment later, he was in front of me, handing me a bottle of water and two tablets.

I smiled gratefully and immediately swallowed the painkillers, hoping they'd fend off the hangover I could already feel brewing. Enjoying the cool water chasing them, I took another gulp before forcing myself to stop. My mission was not to vomit.

"Let me show you where to crash."

Surprise flittered through me when he not only said those words, but he took my hand too, leading me to what I assumed was where I'd be sleeping. We stopped at a closed door. Elijah pointed at it, saying, "This is the bathroom," before continuing on. Two doors later, he opened the door and led me inside, turning on a bedside lamp. It was positioned next to a queen-sized bed. Other than the two bedside tables and the bed, the room was sparse, though there seemed to be a built-in wardrobe. "You gonna be okay?"

"Where's your room?" The question escaped. Something that seemed to happen a lot when I was in the presence of Elijah. It would be easy to blame booze alone, but I knew that wasn't true.

"Next door," he said, his fingers flexing a little, drawing my attention to the fact he was still holding my hand.

I twisted my lips, thinking. It was a good thing, surprising and sweet actually, that the assumption I'd be sharing with him wasn't made. A quick bob of my head followed, and I knew I should simply say goodnight and thanks and proceed to pass out. Apparently, I was destined to not know when to shut the hell up, though.

"I've had too much to drink, but I don't think I'm going to puke." I grimaced, more than aware I wasn't being exactly sexy, talking about spew. "So yeah, um, thank you for driving me home, well, to yours. I like your place, or what I saw. The room's not spinning anymore, so that's a bonus. But, um, you can kiss me goodnight, if you want." I finally stopped speaking, a little breathless and a lot aware I should have stopped speaking after my first word. But my words were out there, and there was no taking them back.

My focus adjusted so I could take in Elijah's reaction fully. I didn't need to squint and took that as a good sign.

Amusement flickered in his eyes, and a smile curved his lips. Those two tells made my shoulders relax. Since I still pulled that smile from him even with all that had passed between us since the night we'd met, I took that as a win. Before me stood a man, so incredibly gorgeous, who had the ability to turn my world upside down, and for the first time, I figured that was just fine by me.

Silence filled the space between us for a couple of beats before Elijah angled towards me. My breath hitched, and then finally, his mouth pressed against mine. It was the slightest of touches before he pulled away, a small curve on his soft lips.

"We'll revisit this tomorrow. Best you head to bed now, Seb." He gave a chin lift towards the door, and with my heart beating like crazy, I simply bobbed my head, stepped into the bedroom, and shut the door behind me.

I leaned against the closed door, my fingers going to my lips, a goofy grin spreading.

Revisit this tomorrow. How on earth was I to sleep with a promise like that?

I stripped out of my clothes, leaving my briefs on, and took another gulp of my water, which I somehow had managed not to spill when my mouth had run away with me and I was kissed.

With the thought of tomorrow on my mind once under the sheets, I smiled, and surprisingly, fell into an easy sleep.

ELEVEN

ELIJAH

I YAWNED around my coffee as I gazed bleary-eyed at the waking world happening outside in my garden. Yesterday had been exhausting. Discovering Tom had passed his phone number to the guy at the bar was a relief. But him admitting that the guy out back, the same man who'd attacked Seb, was his younger brother left me seething and concerned. It had meant long and difficult discussions with both Tom and Drake, who I'd called in when Tom had confirmed it was his brother and his brother's friend.

There was no way I wanted to be involved in family shit, but I couldn't not be. Not only because of the impact on my bar and staff, but also because Tom had explained he wasn't out to his family, nor had they known he worked at Bar QK. It was by chance his brother had found out the truth. Tom confirmed his whole family would disown him should they find out, and his brother was currently using that knowledge to blackmail him while causing shit. His way of making it clear he meant business.

The problem was, I couldn't have this near my customers or my staff, and especially not Seb. And while the knowledge of me all but outing Tom when I'd taken this to Cole and then Drake last night filled me with guilt, it had been the only way to proceed. I was just thankful Tom, between his heartbreaking tears, had given me the green light to call Drake in and was willing to make an official statement.

Drake had indicated it was likely that only a warning could be given, due to the nature of the crimes and assault. But we all hoped that would stop things from escalating, though what it meant for Tom, I didn't know.

Cole had agreed to look out for Tom and had slept over at his place last night. He thought that simply disappearing wouldn't stop anything and hoped that should any retaliation occur, it would likely be at Tom's house and Cole would be able to stop it and scare the pricks away for good.

Only time would tell.

But I was all for it ending.

It would be an excellent exchange for finally starting something up with Seb. Just the thought of him sent a jolt of heat flashing through me. Yesterday, while our kisses had been brief, they'd sent enough awareness through me to know I wanted him. I was tired of denying myself. And more than that, his trust in me, coming to me immediately about Tom, his whole inability to keep a lid on his thoughts, all of it solidified that Seb was worth dropping my guard for.

For the first time in a long while, I wanted more.

No more second-guesses or cold feet.

There was still so much to discover about him, a whole history to share. But more importantly, a whole future to look forward to.

I heard movement and light footsteps heading towards me where I was situated in the dining area of the open-plan space of my home. I was at the table, coffee before me, laptop open. Seb entering had me pulling my gaze in his direction and my smile forming.

Squinty-eyed and messy-haired, he looked particularly dishevelled and equally gorgeous this morning. The bright sunlight poured in through the large, open patio doors to my side, the rays catching the blond in his sun-kissed hair. He was tanned and toned, no doubt from time out in the surf, and so trim and together that an image of me picking the man up and literally carrying him to my bed rushed to me.

I'd never hooked up with a man like him before. Not only a guy with his smaller frame, but also with a man who held my attention so completely.

"Morning," I greeted. "Coffee?"

He brightened a little as he nodded, a smile curving his lips. "That would be great. Thanks."

I stood and indicated for him to sit. He did so, briefly looking down at himself, his cheeks pinkening.

I had no regrets or shame that I'd placed a clean tee out for him this morning in his room. I may have hovered a little too long, peering across at his sleeping form when I'd put the clean T-shirt on the end of the bed. But in my defence, I'd never seen him look so peaceful. While Seb had had a few moments of quiet since we'd met, those times were usually shrouded in upset or contemplation. The majority of time he was a force of nature, virtually buzzing around as he navigated through his tasks. So a sleeping Seb, completely at ease, was a glimpse at a version of the man I didn't know yet.

"How you feeling?" I asked as I flipped the kettle on before grabbing the ground coffee from the fridge.

"Surprisingly okay. Those tablets and water helped." He surveyed the room, taking in the space, and I wondered what he thought of my home. My pad was a labour of love, and with almost every room finally refurnished and modernised, my next focus would be on my garden.

"That's a relief." His eyes connected with mine, and I was happy to see he didn't seem peaky. "Did you find everything you needed in the bathroom?"

He nodded. "Yeah, thanks." Seb's focus moved to the open patio doors.

"We can drink these outside if you want?"

His eyes brightened at the offer. "Thanks. I don't have an outside space, so that'd be great." He stood and ventured over and outside. Meanwhile, I willed the jug to boil so I could join him.

"You want something to eat?" I called out to him.

He glanced over his shoulder back at me and shook his head. "I'm fine, thanks."

I bobbed my head in understanding and turned

back to the steaming kettle, happy it finally clicked off.

"You need a hand?" Seb's voice floated over through the doorway, making me smile. It was quite possibly weird that I liked the sound of his voice in my space, especially in the morning, but having his company was nice, and something I could happily get used to.

"Do you want to grab yourself a mug from the glass-fronted cabinet and my half-empty one from the table?"

Immediately, he went to task, collecting the mugs, asking, "This it?"

"Yeah," I answered, pouring the hot water into the coffee carafe and picking it up, along with a spoon and the milk from the fridge.

Once settled outside, sitting on chairs around the small table overlooking my large yard, I relaxed and topped up my mug after filling up Seb's.

"Thanks for letting me crash."

I glanced over at Seb, offering him a smile. "No worries. Thanks for handling everything so well yesterday," I offered.

A tentative smile appeared on his lips. "How'd it go? Did you get everything sorted that you needed to?" Seb blew on his coffee and took a small sip, wincing slightly on contact.

"Yeah, or as much as I can. Tom's innocent—"

"Oh, that's great. Shit, I feel bad for—"

I shook my head, saying, "No, it's all good. The guy's his brother." Seb's eyes widened. "Yeah, took me by surprise too. There's a whole shitshow of bigotry and bullshit in his family."

"Christ, is he okay?"

"I think sort of relieved that things are out in the open, but I think he's shit scared too."

"Well, his brother didn't bash me, but what he did was pretty violent."

My brows dipped low. My anger at the memory at the forefront. "It was, and I don't know just how far his family would push it, but Cole's looking out for him."

A huff of breath escaped Seb. "That's good. I know how shitty it is to have no one." I stilled as he spoke, hearing the traces of hurt in his matter-of-fact tone. "Cole seems like a good guy."

I bobbed my head, saying, "He is," while my concern for Seb and all he'd been through ate at me. He'd previously told me about his parents, about his whole family turning their backs on him. There were too many shitty excuses for human beings in this world.

"Just let me know how I can help, and I'll do it. I know how important the bar is to you and would hate for anything to ruin what you've built." Kind eyes peered over at me. "And maybe I'll get to know Tom better."

The man before me was one of the good ones. He brought out a tenderness in me no other man ever had managed before. "I appreciate that, thanks, Seb." I bobbed my head, my eyes drifting to his hand on the table, wishing I had the nerve to reach out and hold his hand, and not sure why I was doubting myself. Instead, I continued, "Tom's not due in again until early next week, so I need to figure out what's going on with him and how the police plan on handling the situation." I expelled a heavy sigh, the tiredness from yesterday and my poor sleep catching up with me, despite the early hours.

"Perhaps you could pretend to get me trained up or something and if the police want me to be shadowing Tom or whatever so I'm there in case his brother approaches him?" Seb shrugged. "I could totally wear a wire," he said, his eyes widening. "When I was a kid, there was a whole summer I was determined I wanted to join the FBI. I was all over it, watching movies, memorising moves and lines," he rushed out, making me smile. "It was then this arsehole kid at school took great delight in crapping on my dreams, saying I had to be American and not Australian to join. Was pretty bummed there for a while." An almost whimsical sigh escaped him. "I would have nailed the whole black suit, crisp white shirt, and shades look." A grin stretched his face as he looked over at me. "Even better if I could have been an agent in the Men in Black." He followed with a slight laugh, the sound light and lifting my mood. "But whatever you need, I'll do it."

At his words, his vocal, sweet support, I finally reached out and touched his hand. Seb startled slightly as I caught him by surprise. His reaction morphed quickly to a tender smile that had me mirroring his expression, especially when he turned his hand palm up so he could hold mine.

"I don't think any of that is necessary, even though I'm sure you'd look incredibly hot in a suit." His cheeks pinked at my words. "At the moment, we'll just carry on as usual and hope everything is resolved soon."

Seb bobbed his head. "I'm sure it will be." His eyes brightened, and he sat a little taller, his hand remaining in mine. "And can I just say, holy shit! Lady Bra Ga is incredible."

Happiness filtered through me at his reaction. Seb was lightness and enthusiasm and sunshine. Yeah, there'd been those slivers of something not so carefree, which was more reassuring than everything. It made him more human, more accessible, especially to a guy like me. "You enjoyed the show?"

He nodded enthusiastically. "The best. I've seen movies, but never a live show. I loved every minute."

"She is an amazing performer. Her act's been with us for over a year now. She pulls in the crowds. We have a few other performers who are great in their own right, but, yeah, she's a draw card."

Seb appeared riveted as I spoke, his attention on every word. I cleared my throat a little, uncomfortable, not quite sure how to respond to his rapt attention. He did that a lot, seemed solely focussed on my every word, every syllable. It wasn't like I wasn't used to holding court when needed, but Seb's attention was different. It felt like he was truly listening, as in hearing me while looking into my soul or some shit. As unnerving as that was, I'd be a fool to not latch on to the man who was clearly under my skin.

"I can see why," he said. "Why she pulls in such a crowd," he clarified.

I offered a smile and was about to speak when a rumble had him turning red and clutching his stomach. "Well, that makes the next step clear. Breakfast. My treat."

"Are you not busy?"

I really was, but I'd blown him off one too many times, and I wasn't quite sure how many more chances Seb would give me. The promise I'd given him last night fluttered into my mind unbidden. And I had no desire to back down. But breakfast first. "I have time for breakfast with you."

The slight tension in his shoulders loosened at my words, and I realised his question had been genuine rather than a flippant question intended to placate. "Come on." I stood and offered my hand to him. A flick of his gaze to my hand, then my face, reflected his sweet surprise. He took it almost hesitantly, and I tugged gently, helping him stand. "Do you need me to take you home for a change of clothes first, or are you good?"

"I'll make do." Seb's eyes were bright and wide as he looked up at me.

"Great. Go grab a shower, and I'll tidy up. Fifteen minutes long enough?"

He bobbed his head and made to leave, but I

didn't let go of his hand. Shock registered in his eyes when he glanced at me.

I leaned down slowly, making my intentions clear. His breath hitched while my pulse sped up. There was a slight angling of his head, a tilting of his neck, giving me the all clear. I pressed my lips against his, just a gentle touch before pulling away.

Eyes closed, cheeks flushed, Seb was all kinds of adorable. My gaze roamed his face, recognising a vulnerability I hadn't seen before. I leaned back while simultaneously reaching out and touching his cheek. His eyes sparked open.

"I didn't see you coming." The words slipped out, taking me by surprise, and Seb too from his wide eyes. Before I could backtrack or simply clear my throat and run, his quiet words stopped me.

"Is that a bad thing?"

I shook my head, not quite sure of how to answer but wanting to make it clear that I could never associate Seb with anything bad.

He relaxed at my gesture, tenderness entering his eyes. "I didn't see you coming either." His lips were on mine for the barest of seconds following his words before he spun around and darted back inside my home, leaving me outside and trying to figure out how to even begin to navigate a relationship, specifically one that would stick.

After breakfast, where we'd laughed discussing waves that had knocked us about, I'd dropped Seb off at home, sharing another short and soft kiss with him and promising to call him this evening. Fully aware we needed to talk more openly about what exactly we were doing, especially considering he worked for me and I didn't want to stuff that up for him, I invited him over for food tomorrow—after we'd finished up with the fire department.

I spent some time at work doing the books but wasn't scheduled to be behind the bar at all so was able to hide out for a couple of hours before I was found by Lenny.

"You kept your being here quiet," he said with a quirk of his brow. "Impressive, Boss Man, but you're just the person I was looking for." His smile slipped, and he stepped fully into my office, closing the door behind him.

"What's up?" Immediately concerned by Lenny's reaction, I pulled my brows together.

He sat down heavily in the chair opposite my desk, appearing increasingly ruffled. "My friend Val just called, like five minutes ago. He was here last night." A huff of agitated breath escaped him before he continued, "He called to tell me last night when he left, a couple of guys jumped him."

My muscles tensed immediately, nausea battling it out with the fury building in my gut. "Fuck, is he okay? Does he know who they were?"

Lenny winced. "He will be. Took a couple of punches before a passing car pulled over. And other than it being a couple of young guys, there was nothing more really. Said they looked a little rough but he'd never seen them before."

"Fuck." I wiped a hand over my face. "Did—"

"There's more." A grimace followed his interruption. "He said it was a targeted attack. That they mentioned Bar QK and a whole host of disgusting shit." Lenny's skin flushed red with the heat of his anger. "The guy who pulled over called the police and the ambulance."

I blanched. "He needed to go to the hospital?" This was not good. The poor guy. I knew only too well how intimidating and scary an attack like that could be. It had happened to me when I was much younger. That shit right there was what needed to be taken more seriously in this screwed-up world we lived in.

"No. The paramedics checked him out. He was

fine but shaken. He's made a statement, so I thought you should have the heads-up."

I nodded in appreciation. I didn't think I was jumping the gun to expect Tom's brother, Ricky, to be the culprit. The attack happening at the end of the night could have easily been before the police pulled him on Tom's statement, assuming that had happened last night.

"You okay?" Lenny's tentative voice reached me, managing to break through the pounding in my ears. "You look like you're going to explode. Shit, you're not going to have a heart attack, right?"

I flicked my gaze at him. "You good here if I head out?"

He nodded in acknowledgement.

"You need me to call Cole and organise a guy to be here? You worried?"

Lenny shook his head. "No, I'm fine, honestly. If I'm worried, I'll call Cole, and if anything happens, I'll call the cops."

I switched off my computer, grabbed my keys, helmet, and jacket, and made my way to leave. I paused before exiting fully, turning back to Lenny, who stared at me wide-eyed. "Thanks for coming to me with this." Without waiting for his response, I headed to my bike.

The only person I could go to was my brother-in-law again. He'd be pissed that I kept disturbing him while off-duty, but I needed the connections to be laid out nice and clear. I sighed, beyond livid. Someone being hurt because of drinking at my bar made me sick to my stomach. For years I'd worked so bloody hard to get something amazing going at Bar QK, making it a safe place for the community, and I couldn't let these fucking bigoted bogans take that away from me. I just hoped like hell the police could do their jobs and take these bastards down.

TWELVE

SEB

A RESTLESS SLEEP meant I'd woken bleary-eyed and feeling even worse than my hungover state the previous morning. Rather than booze being the cause, it was me waiting up, checking my phone so often I was sure I had RSI, and waiting for the call from Elijah that never came.

The tingle from his parting kiss became a ghost of a memory as my brain jumped to the very real possibility that he regretted the kiss, the talks, regretted opening himself to something more with me.

There was also the very real possibility he was caught up in the nightmare exploding at work. Bar QK was more than a job to him, more than "just" a business, but my own history was hard to shake off and ignore.

From an early age, I'd soon worked out survival meant you relied on yourself and shouldn't expect anything from anyone. Well, only the bad and the bullshit. But this time I'd hoped Elijah was different. In the depths of my gut, there remained a flicker of awareness that I was being oversensitive. But to nurture that flame took hope and bravery and a whole heap of faith. And if it became clear that my suspicion of his regret was accurate, I had no idea if I could handle it like all the times in my past.

But it was almost time for me to catch my bus and head to the bar, regardless of receiving a call or not. I'd made a commitment to be there when the inspection was taking place, and I needed any chance of making additional money I could get.

I didn't have a game plan for when I arrived. I considered it during the whole journey, but figured I'd simply play it by ear. However I reacted to whatever I discovered would be real and instinctive, and I had no energy to change that.

The front doors were locked, so I made my way around the back. The door was open, the back entry quiet when I stepped inside. I always found places like bars to have a weird, almost lonely feeling to them when they were empty and the lights were off. It perhaps didn't help that it felt a little eerie too.

The sound of bottles clanging together followed by a light thud drew my attention to the main bar. I headed in that direction, my gaze landing immediately on Elijah. He flicked his attention my way instantly, standing straight after rearranging the crates.

"Hi." I followed with an awkward wave that had me inwardly cringing. "It's weird, right, when this place is all closed up. Feels like a place for lost souls or something." I paused briefly, my brain whirling in confusion, trying to figure out what on earth I was talking about. Place for lost souls? What even is that? "So, yeah." I glanced at the time, relieved it was almost ten. "They should be here—" The knock on the front door made me pause and a relieved exhale rushed out of me. "I'll get that," I said quickly, more than aware I hadn't left Elijah room to speak, not even to say hello.

During my rambling, though, it was impossible to not notice the slight tilting of his head, the two lines forming between his brows, but giving him time to speak would have made everything so much worse. Especially if those words had been ignoring the connection we had or even worse, asking to "talk."

I shuddered at the thought, a new sense of resolve settling in me as I unlocked the bar door. I'd keep ignoring my own awkwardness for as long as possible and simply deal when I was forced to. It seemed like I had a plan after all.

I pulled the door open wide, my brows shooting high when my gaze landed on the tall man in the doorway. He was a good half a foot taller than me, his brown hair buzz cut and suiting him perfectly while showcasing the most spectacular green eyes I'd ever seen. Unable to stop myself, I let my eyes roam downwards, resting a moment on the local fire station emblem on his snug-fitting T-shirt and a pair of jeans that I was sure were Wranglers.

It gave him a bit of a weird cowboy vibe that was unusual since the beach was a stone's throw away. But hell if it didn't suit him.

"Sebastian?" he said, his voice smooth and giving me goosebumps.

I nodded, remained mute, and stuck out my hand after he reached for it.

"Benji," he said. "We chatted by email."

"Yes, right." My smile followed, and I felt my

cheeks heat. "Your eyes are the most amazing colour," I blurted. Benji laughed lightly, and I clamped my mouth shut and then quickly released his hand, realising I was still clinging to him.

"Thanks. A gift from my grandad," he said, raising his brows in expectation.

I simply stood there and jumped when heat hit my back in the form of Elijah's hand. "Oh, right, sorry, come on in," I said quickly. I shifted out of the way, losing Elijah's touch, which did something extra to befuddle my brain even more. Benji was hot as hell. It was impossible to not drool over the bloke, but one touch from Elijah sent an awareness through me the likes I'd never experienced before.

And hot didn't even begin to cover just how gorgeous I thought Elijah was. Yeah, he had this whole funky city, grunge vibe thing going, which helped with the sexy factor. But pull off his beanie, and his chestnut hair somehow brought out the deep brown in his eyes even more. He had the ability to render me speechless and frozen with a simple glance. Add into that his care and sweetness, and completely ignoring the mixed messages he'd sent my way, I had no doubt that he was way out of my league.

But damn, I wanted him. All of him.

He could do with his own manual. And not one of those confusing ones you got with IKEA furniture. The ones that had you ignoring them and making a desk look like a bookcase.

No, Elijah's needed to be detailed and thorough and clue a guy in to how to peel back the layers to figure out… well, everything. I'd gladly give up all my vices of Chinese takeout and cheap wine and save hard if I had to.

"What, sorry?"

Elijah saying my name jolted me back to the bar and my perhaps enviable position of standing next to two incredibly delicious men.

His brows were drawn low. "Are we ready to get started?"

"Yes, sure." I nodded, needing to get my head in the game. All ogling aside, this was serious, and passing it was essential to stay open.

We set up in the bar rather than cramming in the office as we worked our way through all of the documentation, showing Benji the previous four years' worth of records and talking through how we'd implemented the recent changes imposed by the Queensland government.

Elijah had gone and made us coffees while I

answered Benji's questions and showed him the relevant information. When he'd returned with three steaming hot mugs, he settled on the bench seat next to me rather than the chair opposite, taking me by surprise.

I side-eyed him while Benji had his head buried in paperwork, wishing I knew what Elijah was thinking. Him not calling me yesterday had stumped me, sure, and our weirdness this morning didn't help. Even though I was fully aware I was responsible for this morning's greeting and strange behaviour.

The need to speak and break the quiet rode me hard as the tension spiked between us. The heat from his body so close to mine made it impossible to be at ease. I willed myself to clamp my mouth shut, worried my words would spill out unfiltered.

Instead, I focussed on Benji—the safer option, considering my vibrating need to touch Elijah, kiss him, or simply rush out my words asking what was going on. "Everything looking okay?" I said, aware my voice didn't sound even.

My words appeared to take the good-looking man by surprise as he jerked his head up. A smile settled on Benji's mouth. "Yeah, all good so far. Sorry this whole process is a ball ache, but there's no cutting corners with fire safety."

I bobbed my head. "For sure. The preventative stuff I imagine is the preferred way forward rather than dealing with fires."

"Too right." His warm gaze roamed my face a moment while I tried to figure out what else to say.

"Uhm, so, just this and a walk around?"

"Yep. Should only be an hour or so. Then I can get out of your hair. There's meant to be a swell coming in this arvo."

Interest piqued and feeling the comfort of a familiar topic, my easy grin settled on my mouth. "Oh, excellent. You surf locally?"

"There's a few local spots I like to head to. It's all just about choosing the right one so I'm not dodging the tourists, you know?"

I nodded. "It's why I prefer to head out super early when I manage to get out."

"I plan to head to Coolum this afternoon. If you're not working—"

"We have plans." Elijah's interruption took me by surprise. It took a moment for his words to register, but when they did, my body heated, a bubble of happiness chasing the path of the spreading warmth.

"Oh, sure. Another time maybe," Benji said gracefully, his gaze roaming over the two of us.

Admittedly, if I were him, I'd be confused too. Not wanting to get my hopes up about Elijah's declaration—but I totally did and embraced the glow of his interruption with fierce hands—it had been clear he was staking his claim on me. Me! Elijah was gorgeous and cool and had this whole sexy boss vibe going for him, and I was just me.

I didn't ever go searching for an ego boost. I was a decent-looking guy, but I was also small and slim, which was regularly held against me. There was also no way in hell I'd ever pass as straight. I'd known that since I was fifteen, or maybe even twelve from the constant jabs from kids at school, but at twelve, I hadn't fancied anyone, so the jibes had never stuck. I tended to attract pricks—as in idiots who thought they were better than me and assumed they could treat me like crap or less than. A few bears had also taken a liking to me, but big brutes of men tended not to appeal to me.

I risked a glance at Elijah, whose head turned a moment after my own. His gaze connected with mine, a heat there that I'd seen yesterday. Then his lips curved upwards, and I inhaled fully, quite possibly for the first time since arriving at work.

I dragged my attention away to refocus on Benji. It would be too easy to drool over the perfection of Elijah. When I did so, the firey was still looking at the both of us, a small smile lifting his lips. And Elijah's thigh then pressed against mine, and that long breath I'd enjoyed escaped me instantly.

The urge to lean into him, reach out to touch him niggled at me. An hour, I reminded myself. After that, we'd talk, and hopefully he'd make good on the more he'd promised me a couple of nights ago.

Somehow, I managed to finish off answering the final few questions Benji had without getting too distracted. And after leading him around so he could check our compliance and that we were up to spec, it was finally time to say goodbye, thankfully after receiving the appropriate certification.

"No," he said as I led him to the front door. Elijah had disappeared about fifteen minutes earlier to take a call. "I can't believe I haven't seen her act. I've been here quite a few times and managed to catch a few shows, but never hers."

I may have started chatting enthusiastically on our tour of the bar about the drag show and Lady Bra Ga's incredible performance. But as far as I was concerned, everybody needed to see it.

"You must. There's a performance schedule

online, both social media and the website, so be sure to check it out."

A genuine grin was sent my way. "I definitely will, Seb."

I reached for the lock and unbolted the door, ready to show him out. His words had me pausing.

"So, you and Elijah are a thing?" Curiosity filled his gaze while I felt a little stumped, not quite sure how to answer.

"Um, well, he's my boss." Benji's brow quirked high in challenge. I rolled my eyes. "We've spent some time together." I wanted nothing more than to say we were "something," but a couple of kisses and the promise of dinner wasn't exactly something I could label.

"So it would or wouldn't be a problem if I asked you out sometime?"

My eyes sprang wide open. "Me?" The question came out unbidden, the word wrapped up in disbelief, causing me to blush and Benji to frown.

"Yes, Seb. You."

I pulled my lips tight and pressed them between my teeth, wondering what was going on with the gorgeous men in the world acting so weirdly.

"So," he said, "would it?"

My heart flipped over, knowing full well the

answer. "It would be," I admitted. "A problem," I clarified to be sure. "Thank you, though."

A tilt of his head made him seem even more stupidly sexy. I really needed him to leave. While there was no way I'd be changing my mind about Elijah, so much handsome around me addled my brain.

"Good choice," he said with a wink, and reached and shook my hand. "A drink between friends at the next show would be good though."

"Definitely," I said, relieved I hadn't offended him.

With the door wide, he turned to go before angling around a little. He lifted his hand in the air, calling out, "See you, Elijah." Another wink was then sent my way, along with an expression filled with mischief.

I grimaced, having no doubt from his reaction that Elijah had stepped into the room at some point while I'd been talking. With no way of avoiding it, I pushed the door closed, locked it, and turned around.

Elijah stood behind the bar, hands pressed on the wooden surface, his gaze intent and zeroed in on me. "Hey," I said, my shoulder lifting a little. "So, have you got things to do or—"

"I think it was a good choice too."

His words stopped me short and sent my heart pounding. I swallowed hard, my mouth going dry. After a beat, I managed, "Me too."

His smile was disarming, and when he stepped from behind the bar and headed purposefully in my direction, I just hoped like hell he'd only stop once his lips were pressed against mine.

And oh, how they did.

He teased my mouth open, unrelenting and soft, a quiet urgency in the movement. Responding immediately, I clung onto him, needing the connection so I didn't float away. Our tongues connected, and a zap of heat licked a path over my skin. My groan escaped, raw and instinctive. The sound caused him to pull away, but only for his lips to travel my jaw to my neck. I groaned once more, loving the hungry kisses on my skin.

"Holy shit, can I pull up a chair?"

Lenny's voice had Elijah tearing his mouth from me. Thankfully, I maintained my grip so I didn't fall flat at the loss.

Elijah turned towards the bar and Lenny's voice, allowing me to get a visual on him too. Elbows on the bar, hands cupping his chin, his eyes were wide, and a huge smirk settled on his lips.

"The back door was unlocked. I did call out from back there. I now understand why you didn't hear me." Amusement danced in his eyes as his gaze flicked between the two of us. "You want me to leave so you can go at it?"

Mortification battled with amusement, and laughter threatened to burst free. My lips twitched as Elijah sighed, his hand replanting itself around me. My own sigh escaped at the move, and I didn't care that it made both men look in my direction. A quick glance up at Elijah had my heart fluttering. Heat remained in his eyes, and his own small smirk twitched his lips.

He looked at Lenny. "We're just leaving."

Lenny snorted, standing up straight. "Spoilsports."

"You okay to head out?" Elijah asked me.

"Definitely." I slipped my hand into his, loving the touch and how his palm felt in mine.

"I totally called it," Lenny said, beginning to move around the bar, preparing for the day.

I glanced over in question.

"You two getting together."

"I don't want to know," Elijah said, his voice turning grumbly. "You're the worst bunch of gossips."

"I can take ownership of that," he said, laughing and making me snort.

"Your friend Val," Elijah said, "how's he doing?"

Not sure who Val was or what the problem was, I glanced first at Elijah and noticed the concern etched on his face. When Lenny spoke, I turned my attention back to him. The humour there a moment ago had disappeared.

"He's okay. No longer shaken, which is great. Just pissed off and angry. He's made of tough stuff, so he won't let this get him down. He said you were there at the police station and helped him out."

"What happened?" I asked.

"You don't kn—"

"Shit, I'm sorry," Elijah said, cutting Lenny off. "And I didn't call you yesterday." He angled more in my direction and squeezed my hand. Guilt filled his gaze and then something else slipped in and replaced that emotion. "You were worried." His voice dipped low, sounding pissed off. "I should have called, but yesterday was a clusterfuck."

Surprise and relief rushed out of me, my own understanding registering. "It's okay. Why don't we get out of here, and you can catch me up?"

Elijah's gaze didn't waver as he said, "I can do

that." A small exhale followed his words, and I was happy I'd offered him some relief.

"Thanks, Lenny, just call if you need anything." He threw Lenny a nod, and we left with me offering a quick goodbye.

THIRTEEN

ELIJAH

OVER LUNCH I'd explained everything that had happened with Val. Including how Ricky had been arrested yesterday afternoon after Val had IDed him. They'd also arrested a guy called Rocky.

After that, Cole and I had spent some time making sure that Tom was okay while trying to prepare for any possible repercussions. I went on to explain how I'd also been at the station for Val, and by the time I'd got home, it had been late and I'd been burned out.

I was pleased I'd gone though. There was a part of me that felt responsible for the attack on Val, so being there to make sure he was well taken care of mattered. I also told Seb how Drake would be calling at some point to get him to ID Ricky for the paint attack, which Seb readily agreed to.

"I just can't believe it," Seb said with a shake of his head. "I'm relieved this Val guy is okay, though."

"Yeah, me too. He was keen to press charges."

"It's amazing how many people don't."

The reality made my chest heat in frustration. "I know. It's shit. I'm just glad it didn't turn out that way this time."

Seb's gentle gaze roamed over my face, and he reached out and touched my arm. "It was really good of you to go and check on Tom." His touch combined with his compliment brought heat of a different kind to my chest and gut. "Is he going to be okay? What about his family? You said they didn't know he was pan, right?"

I nodded and removed his hand so I could hold it, earning me a smile. "Not sure if his brother has told anyone anything. The good thing is that Ricky's received a couple of cautions before, so Drake seems to think the judge may come down harder on him, plus he's in remand rather than being released on bail. They'll find out in a couple of weeks."

While taking a drink, Seb listened intently. When he finished and placed his glass of water down, he tilted his head. "I was a dick earlier, when I arrived at the bar."

Guilt flared to life as I shook my head. "I get it. I said I'd call. And you weren't a dick so much as a scared rabbit or some shit." Somehow I managed to smile. Knowing why he'd avoided me and thinking back to how jumpy he'd been was kinda funny, but only now that he was holding my hand and sounding ridiculously cute with his apology.

He snorted. "Maybe, but I jumped to conclusions and considered running."

My body tensed at that, all too aware of his practically nomad past of picking up and trying new places to live. The thought of him skipping out sat heavily. "You'd have run as in left?" I didn't intend for my voice to come across so hard, but his flinch at my tone told me it had been just that. "Shit, sorry." I huffed out a heavy breath. "Listen, this talking shit can be seriously overrated. Just..." I hesitated, searching Seb's face and reading some sadness and uncertainty there. It was clear he was just as terrified as I was. I tried again. "Just, if you think this isn't for you and you think you're gonna up and leave anytime soon, I need to know." I felt like a dick, putting myself out there like this, but a shot for

something real with Seb was worth the embarrassment licking its way through me.

Surprise rippled through me when Seb released
my hand, stood, and stepped around the table. His
eyes were wide, and a flush steadily rose from his
neck to his cheeks. "Scoot back," he said, a small
shake to his voice.

I did so immediately, my surprise changing to
awareness.

With my chair shifted, my breathing stuttered
when he straddled my thighs, his chest close, his arse
landing directly on my groin. Immediately, I gripped
him, keeping him steady, both hands on the small of
his back.

In this position, we were almost eye to eye. Our
lips within touching distance with the slightest of
movements.

"You terrify me." The quiet words pressed against
me. "But in the best of ways." Emotion swirled in his
eyes, and my dick twitched. "I don't plan on leaving.
I want us to see where this is going."

And those were the words I needed.

A shift of my hands followed—one to his arse to
pull him closer, the other to the back of his head so I
could finally get a taste.

Warm and supple lips pressed against mine. The

movement was slow, the press just the right side of sweet and perfect. His words ran through my head as I flicked my tongue out, chasing a better taste. Finally, we were on the same page. The knowledge slammed into me, and I tugged him closer, both of us groaning around our touching mouths when he ground against me.

The sound of his need colliding with mine ratcheted up my desire to claim this man. It didn't matter that I had no idea what that meant at this moment. The claiming of his mouth, this kiss, was a start.

Our lips clashed, moving quicker, almost to the point of frenzy. I wanted everything Seb would give me. The swipe of his tongue against mine had me squeezing his arse cheek. His hips jerked, the push he needed to start rubbing against my cock.

I pulled away, breathless as he ground down on me, desperately wanting our clothes out of the way. My hand went to his jeans, my eyes on his button and zip as I quickly undid both. When he whimpered, I lifted my gaze. His bottom lip clamped between his teeth kicked up my need.

"Don't stop," he said on a gasp, and I realised my hand had paused before reaching inside to find the skin I craved.

I managed to smile through my lust and moved my fingers that were so close to his backside.

"What—" Wide-eyed, he cut himself off and held on tight when I stood.

Fuck, this was the first time I'd picked up any man this way. He felt so right in my arms, perfectly positioned for so many tantalizing possibilities, but for now, I wanted my bed.

"Bed okay?" I asked, pretty sure I was reading him well enough to know it was what he wanted.

Relief sagged his shoulders, and he bobbed his head quickly, making me laugh. He shut that down when he clamped his mouth on my neck and pushed against my groin.

"Urgh… keep that up and the table will have to do." The gruffness of my voice was full of need.

"But lube and condoms," he said between kisses. "I can't imagine you have any here."

I throbbed in my jeans at the mention of both. I had no expectations beyond getting my hands and my mouth on him; his mention of more had me holding on to him even tighter and walking at a fast pace through the house to my bedroom.

He was grinning by the time he pulled away to look at me as I placed him on the bed.

"What's that smile for?" I asked breathily.

"Your eagerness is hot."

I chuckled and lowered towards him, hand on his waist and edging him further up the bed. "That's not the only thing that's hot." I trailed my lips down his neck and reached down to the hem of his T-shirt. Seb hastily helped me remove it.

Smooth, soft skin clinging to his defined muscles greeted me. No muscles here were from weights. Rather, they were the result of the hours of surfing he enjoyed. Seb pulling at my own tee dragged my eyes away from his chest. I tugged it off before lowering myself for another kiss.

Urgency pressed and moved our lips together, the desire to sear the moment into my memory urging me on more.

Seb was heat and fire and returned my kisses with equal fervour.

"Jeans," he said on a gasp as he moved his mouth from mine.

I grinned and shifted, working on tearing off the rest of my clothes while he did the same. As I tugged at my jeans, I froze momentarily, my eyes zeroing in on his erection. It lay heavy on his stomach, leaving wetness on his skin.

"Fuck," I mumbled, rushing forward to get naked. Any hint at distance or even pretending he didn't affect me broke off and dissolved completely. I needed him to know how much I wanted him. When he moved his hand and it glided over his stomach to his balls and he tugged, I edged closer, my eyes flicking to his.

Eyes partially concealed by half-lowered lids stared back at me. Once again, Seb's lower lip was held between his teeth. He lay there almost expectantly, definitely needy, but almost frozen and clearly waiting for my move.

The knowledge calmed me a little, forcing me to slow down. As far as I was concerned, this was the start of something new, was just the beginning. The urgency still beat at me, but there'd be more times than this, and from the hint of uncertainty in his eyes, he needed to know all of that.

I'd start by showing him.

Reaching out, I trailed my fingers up his calves and to his thighs. The breath of air that escaped him was choppy. It also had Seb releasing his lip and a smile curving his mouth. I eyed my bedside drawer a moment before returning my attention fully to the man before me.

"Do I need to get a rubber to suck you off?" I didn't care if I did. It would have been nice to taste him, but there'd be time for that if we had to wait.

His already flushed cheeks pinkened more, and he shook his head. "No, only if you want to." He angled up onto his elbows. "I have regular checks, and it's been a while."

A shot of pleasure and relief went through me at his words. "Me too," I said before swiping my tongue across by bottom lip. "I'm good to go without when sucking you off."

Air whooshed out of him as he all but gasped, "Okay. I'm good with that too."

A smirk tilted my lips as I backed away and lowered myself between his legs. His eyes stayed on me as he remained leaning on his elbows. The flick of my gaze in his direction was the precursor to showing him just how much I wanted him. I made sure to maintain eye contact as I dipped out my tongue and gave one long, hard lick along his length.

His garbled, "Holy shit," egged me on. This time, I went for it.

By the time I lapped my tongue gently against his slit, then preceded to bob, suck, and lick, Seb had fallen flat on the mattress, his back arching and the hottest pleas for me to never stop falling from his lips.

His cries had my balls tightening. I reached out and cupped his sac, tugging and rolling lightly. In response, one of his hands clamped down on my head and fisted the short strands of my hair. A loud gasp was followed by him calling out my name, and then he went rigid, spilling into my mouth. I swallowed quickly, not wanting to lose a drop, then licked and bobbed a few more times just as his limbs relaxed and he released his tight grip.

I pulled away, my one hand still gently on the base of his cock. I held him as I lapped a couple of times on the end. His groan and shudder followed, then he lifted his head. His pupils were blown, cheeks red, and lips puffy from biting down on them. He'd never looked hotter or so damn fucking cute.

"I can't feel my toes," he said breathlessly, a small smile following.

As I carefully released him from my grip, I eased up to reach his mouth, rubbing my hard cock along his legs on the way, stopping when my length pressed between his thighs.

"That was incredible." His words were earnest, almost awed, and hell if happiness didn't flush through me and make me feel awesome.

Instead of answering, I pressed my mouth to his, loving the way he groaned again and wrapped his arms tightly around me, holding me close. The kiss was languid, tender, and despite me being rock-hard, I was more than happy to slow things down.

I pulled away and was greeted with Seb's relaxed gaze. Contentment drifted through me knowing I'd put that expression on his face. He reached up and threaded his fingers through my hair, the touch tender and unexpectedly familiar.

"Can we shower?" he asked, his voice quiet, sounding blissed out.

I grinned, searching his face. "Do you now have feeling in your feet? Can you manage the walk?"

He chuckled. "I think so. Though you carrying me…." His dick twitched against my stomach, and his breathing changed.

"You like that, huh?"

I nodded. "Didn't think I would, but you doing it was hot as hell."

My cock throbbed in response to his breathy answer. "There are so many things I'd like to do with you in my arms," I admitted, the possibilities flashing in my mind.

Wide eyes burst open at my words. "Yeah?"

"Oh yeah."

Seb grinned at that, looking thoroughly on board with the possibility.

"But shower first," I said.

We stood, my cock sticking out long and proud, enjoying Seb's eyes as his gaze lowered, widened, and even more when he swiped his tongue over his bottom lip. My hard-on jerked in response, earning a new sort of smile from Seb.

He remained quiet as we headed to the shower, the silence far from awkward. Once under the heat of the water, we soaped up, and I exhaled in relief when his soap-sudded hands closed around my erection.

"Lean against the wall," Seb said.

I did so quickly, up for whatever he offered. He rose onto the balls of his feet, his mouth moving to reaching distance once I dipped lower for him. Hungrily, he slid his lips against mine. I accepted the kiss eagerly, wrapping my arms around him so we were flush—or as flush as possible with his hand working me over. Seb teased my mouth, my tongue, owning the kiss... owning my cock. Satisfaction thrummed through me at the possession.

The gasp tore from me when he eased back. I had a moment to grumble, trying to seek out his mouth, but then I tilted my head back against the wall when his lips met my chest. He licked his way down, nipping my skin on his way, or I desperately hoped, to putting his mouth on my cock.

A small movement alerted me to him washing off the suds, and my stomach tightened in anticipation. And then I was engulfed in perfect heat. Unable and unwilling to keep my hands to myself, I reached down, my gaze following the movement so I could watch him.

With his eyes on me, intensity in their depth, I throbbed, swelling in his mouth, causing the both of us to moan. Receiving head was generally fantastic, but Seb worked me over and unravelled me, taking sucking cock to a whole new level of phenomenal.

By the time I groaned my release, spilling and jerking while Seb didn't relent on sucking and licking, my legs threatened to give out.

"Holy fuck." My lids were heavy, my knees genuinely shaking. "I need to sit before I collapse," I admitted with a chuckle.

Seb, looking thoroughly pleased with himself and ridiculously sexy with his plump lips, stood, kissed me quickly, and left the walk-in shower, passing me a towel a few seconds later. "You need help?" Humour and self-satisfaction lifted his words.

I quirked my brow high at him, loving how assured he was. "Just get your arse dry and into my damn bed."

A snort preceded his "But it's only, what, three or something?"

I shrugged as I towelled myself dry. "Don't give a shit. Thought we could spend the rest of the day and night there. You up for that?"

The smile on his face remained in place as he nodded. "Definitely."

FOURTEEN

SEB

THE FOLLOWING WEEK SPED BY—HARDLY surprising as I was on a high of sweet kisses, hot mouth- and-hand action, and evenings spent getting to know Elijah.

Work was work, which meant I was happy going through the motions and trying to be creative when it came to advertising. Carla had decided that since my focus was off the fire audit, I could take over and step up with the social media portion of the bar.

I was all up for it, though I had a lot to learn.

I had a phone and all the usual accounts, but I wasn't really into uploading the details about my own life. While my years on the move had resulted in meeting plenty of new people, there were few I could genuinely call good friends. There was Sid, though, who I really needed to touch base with soon, as I was being slack and hadn't been in contact. And quite possibly there could be Tom.

He'd returned to work on Tuesday, looking surprisingly together and not distraught, which I'd feared. I'd chatted to him about random stuff that day, and the same again on Thursday when I'd been at work, which led me to Friday.

I'd promised a quick drink with him after I'd finished work, aware I had to deliver those leaflets if I wanted to have enough cash to cover a few extras next week.

Elijah had said he'd drop me at my place, and he may have grumbled a time or two when I told him how busy my weekend would be, so sleepovers were unlikely. I'd stayed there every night since last Sunday. While we hadn't had full-on sex yet, there'd been plenty of heated moments, and admittedly, it was Elijah who was slowing us down.

He was being all sweet and considerate, which left me a little confused. It came down to my own insecurities about people, men especially, believing I needed looking after, coddling even, which was so far from the truth.

It wasn't like I was against being cared for; far from it. The concept was awesome, as long as the balance was there. And with Elijah, I thought we could have that. But, between him being my boss, being a helluva lot more financially stable than I was, having an actual two-bedroom house he owned, plus that he was a much bigger guy than I was, well, my insecurities flared to life.

There was also the fact that I was horny. Mouths and hands had their place. Our time together had been spectacular, in fact, but my eagerness to take it to the next step was an understatement.

"You sure you're good to take a break?" I asked Tom as he refilled the fridge, beginning to prepare for the Friday night crowd.

He stood and stretched his back. "I really am. I've been hauling crates all afternoon. Give me a sec."

I nodded and turned on my stool to take in the bar.

It was only mid-afternoon, so the place was quiet. When I'd popped out front earlier, trying my hand at taking a few images for Instagram, there'd been a decent crowd of people having lunch. All that was left now was a few stragglers, clearly tourists, and a few faces I knew as locals. It's one of the things I loved about Bar QK—the local, friendly vibe.

There was a pleasant hum in the room. Quiet conversations, the odd laugh and snicker, and even with the twelve or so people, the atmosphere remained relaxed and friendly. The large concertina doors were wide open, letting in the ocean breeze and the spring sunshine.

Honestly, I had no idea what my future held long-term—even at my age I'd yet to work out my passion—but for right now, I was perfectly content.

"Got you an iced tea," Tom said as he sat beside me, drawing my attention away from the bright sky and to his hazel eyes.

"Thanks," I said, relieved he hadn't bought me booze. "How's your day gone so far?"

He shrugged, taking a drink of what looked to be Coke. "Yeah, good. Busy preparing for tonight." I didn't know Tom well at all, but I knew a look of uncertainty when I saw one.

"You worried about working tonight?"

He shrugged again, this one smaller and not so carefree.

"I get it if you are. It's only been a week, but Cole said he was here, right?"

A slow release of breath escaped when he nodded. "Yeah. Said he'd drop me off home too."

Relief unfurled inside me. I understood the hurt and worry linked to family being homophobic arse-holes, could commiserate with the nerves of trying to carry on as normal while fearing something could happen. It was a crappy way to live. "I'm pleased he has your back."

"I'm grateful," he said, "don't get me wrong, but knowing I have to be babysat...." His lip curled in distaste. "My family already thinks I'm soft. Always stuck out like a sore thumb compared to everyone else." A mirthless laugh followed.

I sighed in understanding. "I get it, I do, but perhaps don't overthink it. Are you close with your family?" I assumed he wasn't, but I could easily have been wrong.

Tom shook his head. "Not really. I've distanced myself, have my own place. I moved out of home as soon as I was able to. I just never fully closed the door, you know?"

I nodded, but not quite knowing since my family had been very vocal about me no longer being part of them. "And now?" I asked, wondering if his brother had outed him or not.

"Not yet, but it's only a matter of time."

"What are you going to do?" I asked, feeling truly sorry for the guy.

He shrugged. "Think I'm at the point where I just need to tell them and deal with the fallout." Tom took a sip of his drink. "But enough about that," he said, shifting a little and clearly over the conversation. "I heard that the hot firey chatted you up on Sunday and the boss man went all caveman and kicked him out."

I snorted, hard, shaking my head, and wondering how on earth he'd heard that since it had only been me and Elijah here. I swore these walls had ears. "That's not what happened. No one was kicked out, and Elijah certainly didn't go all caveman." The memory of his claiming me was pretty damn hot, but there was no way I'd be admitting that.

Disappointment slithered over Tom's features, making me laugh. "Why do you look so disappointed?" Amusement carried my words.

A smile slipped onto Tom's face, the first I'd seen from him over the last few times I'd seen him. "Just thought it would be extra hot."

"Hey, no saying Elijah's hot." I quirked my brow at him. "Even though he so is."

This time a laugh flowed out of Tom. "Ha! Looks like he's not the only one with caveman tendencies." He wiggled his brows, leaving me shaking my head at him.

"What are you being a caveman about?"

Startled, my eyes widened, and I almost hurt my

neck looking over at Elijah so fast. "Uhm, nothing," I said quickly, much to Tom's glee.

"And that's my cue to leave you to it, caveman." Tom picked up his glass, grinned at a confused-looking Elijah, and walked away to get back to work.

"Do I want to know?" Elijah scooted next to me, his thigh pressing against mine. I sighed into the touch, wishing we could do more, but I'd been the ridiculous one to insist there was no unnecessary PDA while at work. Elijah had argued that there was no such thing as unnecessary PDA, and I kinda wished I'd listened to him.

"Nope." I smiled as I spoke, loving the look he gave me.

"You ready to get out of here?"

I nodded. "Yeah."

"And you sure I can't convince you to let me come over later?"

There was no show tonight, which meant it wouldn't be a late one for him, plus I thought he planned to leave in a couple of hours or so. But if he came over, it would mean a late night fooling around, and I really needed to be out by six in the morning so I could get on with my deliveries.

"Maybe tomorrow?" I offered, not liking that I wouldn't get the chance to see him tonight either. "If

I make a really good go of it tomorrow, it means there'll be less for me to do on Sunday, so I can afford the morning distraction I know you'll give me."

Elijah's eyes flickered to my mouth, and my breath hitched, really wanting his lips on mine.

"Car, so I can kiss you." My words came out quickly, breathlessly.

Elijah didn't hesitate to stand, reach out to me, and lead me to his car.

He didn't wait until I was in the passenger seat. Instead, he turned me at the door, pressed me against the metal and glass, and his lips fused with mine.

Was it even possible for kisses to just keep on getting better?

Our mouths melded, tongues swiped, and the desire to say screw my commitments this afternoon was on the tip of my tongue. Each kiss we shared was heady and felt so deliciously right I had no desire to stop them, but....

Reluctantly, I eased out of the kiss. Shallow breaths passed between us, my gaze hazy, his lids at half-mast.

"You really need to go?" A sweet neediness lifted

his question, making me smile and my heart do a happy flip.

"Afraid so, but I promise to work my arse off tomorrow so we can spend the night together."

His gaze roamed mine. "I'd really like that. If I manage to get out of here early, I'll see how you're getting on and perhaps come and help you."

My heart constricted before building up speed at double the pace. "You'd do that for me?"

His smile had my heart stuttering. "Of course."

"But it's delivering leaflets." I had zero shame in how I earned extra cash, but the thought of Elijah assisting created an image that didn't quite sit right for me.

Elijah gently kissed me before saying, "It could be mucking out stalls or washing cars, I don't care. If I can lend a helping hand for the very selfish reason of spending some more time with you, then of course I'll be there."

I grinned widely. "Okay. Sounds good."

BY FIVE O'CLOCK THE FOLLOWING DAY, I HAD completed the largest area of my delivery, amazed at my progress. I grinned, thinking back to Elijah chasing me down a couple of hours earlier, following my instructions about where he needed to go before he'd taken off like a man possessed, very clearly on a mission.

The sound of an engine pulled my attention to the road, a smile lifting my mouth when Elijah headed towards me in his car. He pulled up a few metres away, then exited his vehicle.

"All good?"

I nodded. "Yeah. Think I can stop for the day. I probably have just two or three hours tomorrow left." Elijah opened the boot of his car for me to drop in my now empty bags. After closing it, he tugged me to him, dotting a sweet kiss on my lips.

"That mean I get to take you home?"

"I think you've earned some me time," I sassed, earning me a squeeze on my arse. With a smile on my face, I settled in his car, content with my hand on his thigh as we headed to my small flat.

When we arrived, I dumped the bags on the floor and made my way to the small kitchen area to flip on the kettle. My place was shabby, with well-worn furniture and only a few personal possessions dotted around the place. But it was clean and tidy-ish.

I glanced over at Elijah, seeing him take in my space. It was the first time he'd been here.

When his gaze connected with mine, he smiled. "Cosy," he said, making me smile. It was almost the polar opposite of his home, and that was okay. Having previously house shared, and many times having camped out on sofas and sofa beds in the past, the fact that this place was my own space to kick back and relax in was something I was proud of.

"It does me just fine," I answered. He bobbed his head in response. "I plan to jump in the shower. Thought we could have Chinese takeout if that's okay? You want to order while I get washed up?"

His gaze sharpened. "I could always help you." A salacious smile curved his lips high.

I snorted in response. "I'm hungry, and if you get in my tiny shower with me, we're likely to smash through the glass wall."

"Fine," he grumbled. "What do you want, and I'll call it through?"

"Surprise me." I always went for the same meal, so it was good to mix it up a little.

I left Elijah to it and showered, paying extra attention to prepping myself—ready for our heated nights to be taken to the next level. It was my mission tonight. And getting myself ready so he could go to town on my arse was just stage one of said mission.

Earlier in the week, we'd already shared how we were both vers, much to my relief. My preference was to bottom, which Elijah seemed very happy about, but switching it up and topping scratched that hard-on itch I sometimes had.

That we'd already discussed sex was a good thing, but he'd still held back without telling me why. While he managed to get me off topic by the pair of us blowing our loads, which was all levels of incredible, I wanted him something fierce.

Dressed in boardies and a tee, I headed out of my room after cramming the bedsheets I'd stripped off that morning into my hamper. Clean sheets were on my bed, tucked in and making the small room look tidy.

"The food will be ready in ten," he said when I exited.

"Excellent. We can head out now and walk to get it." I grabbed my keys and bank card, and we left, Elijah clasping my hand.

The two of us walking side by side, Elijah holding my hand, was definitely a couple-y thing I could get used to. I told him so with a grin, earning me a chuckle and a "Me too."

A few moments later, Elijah said, "Harriet's invited us over for a barbie in a couple of weeks, if you're up for it."

I side-eyed him. "She knows we're seeing each other?"

"I told her we're *together*, yes."

I grinned at the emphasis. "You know, she was the one who told me in no uncertain terms that you were attracted to me."

He snorted. "Well, she was the one who told me in no uncertain terms that I was a dickhead for taking so long to pull my head out of my arse and make you mine."

It was no use. With my heart slamming against my rib cage and my breath catching far too dramatically at his words, I halted. He stopped and moved to stand in front of me. My gaze travelled to his face. "Is that what I am?"

There was no doubt what I referred to. Understanding was immediate in the softening of his brown eyes. "I like to think we're each other's."

I leaned in closer, my voice lowering as I said, "Let's seal that tonight, properly." There was so much more I wanted to say, and it was unlike me to clamp my mouth shut and hold back. But explaining how I wanted to ride him hard until he blew my mind, which would then lead to me considering in graphic detail just how the image of the two of us connected would look, was a little too much in public, the door of the takeaway just a few metres away.

When his breathing changed and his eyes became heated, I grinned and pushed myself against him, angling up so he could lean down and kiss me. The touch was quick and firm and all the confirmation I needed that he understood and was on board.

"Do we really need to eat?"

His question had me laughing and so tempted to say screw it. "We'll both need the energy," I said, and his already heated eyes almost glowed with the promise of tonight. "Come on. Let's grab our food, eat, and then you can finally stop being a gentleman and fuck me hard."

The look on his face was comical. And apparently, I wasn't that great at keeping my mouth clamped shut.

I didn't have it in me to care that my words often ran away from me, not when Elijah's gaze turned possessive and he wrapped an arm around me, his head lowering to my neck. "Me doing the right thing by you and making sure you know how real this is between us just changed tacks," he whispered, his tongue lapping at my skin. A groan slipped past my lips. "Your arse is mine." One more lick followed before he pulled away. I stumbled, only remaining upright because his arm was securely around me.

I swallowed hard, then forced myself to look away. "Okay. Food first."

I all but dragged him to Wok Me, where Xiu Mei's smile turned into an open-mouthed gape when her eyes sprang to Elijah, whose hand was possessively at my waist.

"Hey," I said in greeting.

Her surprise turned into delight when she said, "Hey, Seb." She flipped a glance in her dad's direction, whose back was turned as he cooked. Gaze back on me, she lowered her voice. "I was wondering why I hadn't seen you in ages, but now I know."

I rolled my eyes at her, though I didn't hold back my smirk. "This is Elijah. Elijah, Xiu Mei."

"How's it goin'?" Elijah said from beside me.

"Good, thanks. You picking up an order?" Her gaze returned to mine, question there. "Didn't see your usual."

"Geez, I know I'm a creature of habit, but can't a guy mix things up every now and then?"

"Apparently," she sassed, then stood upright, her

voice turning to its normal pitch when her dad moved to the front of the counter with a bag of food that I really hoped was ours.

Interacting with Xiu Mei was great and all, but my dick was still hard, and with Elijah's words still pinging around in my brain, the implication rushing around through my veins, I was desperate to get home.

Her dad bobbed his head in my direction and passed his daughter the bag. She glanced at it. "Elijah, looks like this one's for you."

He stepped from my side, saying, "Thanks," and pulled out his wallet. As if sensing exactly why I was stepping to his side, he focused on me. "I'll get these."

I bobbed my head, absolutely fine with that. There'd be other times I could pick up the bill. The knowledge sent a fresh wave of excitement through me at the certainty that we were officially dating and planned to make this work. "Thanks."

A flicker of surprise appeared in his eyes, which was quickly chased away by something else. Relief, possibly, that I didn't feel the need to argue.

As he paid, Xiu Mei continued to throw glances between us. She practically vibrated with the need to ask questions. I threw her a lifeline. "Perhaps we can catch up for a coffee in the next couple of weeks. You have a break coming up, right?"

With the increased rightness washing over me, the desire to settle and put myself out there urged me on, encouraging me to start building my own network of friends. And it would be good to know someone who wasn't linked to Bar QK.

While Xiu Mei was a few years younger than me and we didn't appear to have that much in common on the surface, I'd liked her from the first time we'd chatted. Her friendship was worth investing in.

"That sounds great." Her attention shifted to Elijah. "It was nice meeting you."

"Yeah, you too," he said before turning, his hand settling on my shoulder.

I threw Xiu Mei a wink as I headed out, then looked up at the man whose heat pressed against me, comfortable and reminding me how letting down my guard could look all kinds of awesome.

FIFTEEN

ELIJAH

WE ABANDONED our food halfway through. Honestly, I was surprised we'd managed so many mouthfuls before I couldn't take it any longer.

Despite Seb being the one to make his intentions and need for me clear, there was no hardship in his desires. I wanted him fiercely. He'd mentioned earlier me holding back and being a gentleman, but that wasn't really it.

Being too damn afraid of jumping in and taking him completely had held me back. In truth, I'd been protecting my damn heart.

I'd never been more relieved to be called out for procrastinating.

My mouth latched to his. I battled with the need to kiss him forever and the desire to wrench myself away so I could open him up and bury myself deep. Seb made the decision for me when he pulled away, gasping for breath.

"I can't wait anymore. I need you too bad."

I kissed him again, unable to resist when he said shit like that to me. He laughed against my mouth, and I angled away, taking in how the lust in his eyes didn't diminish alongside his small chuckle.

Already naked and grinding up against each other, we'd both end up coming if we stayed like this. I eased away, snatching up the lube and the foil wrapper Seb had placed on the side when we'd first entered his room.

The hitch of his breath drew my attention to Seb and the flare of heat in his gaze.

"This what you want?" I asked, my voice raspy.

"You know it."

Seb asking for and taking what he wanted pushed my arousal into overdrive. For all his clumsiness, his inability to rein himself in sometimes, his confidence shone through. I liked even more that it was faith in me that encouraged him to be so open.

Cock sheathed and lubed, fingers slick, I teased him open, dipping in and stretching.

Gasps came free and fast from Seb as I kept a steady pace while my dick throbbed, sure I could get off on this moment right here alone. On my knees, I continued to ease inside him, my other hand moving to his half-mast cock. I smiled, watching his face carefully to make sure he was okay.

It didn't matter how turned on I felt or how good it was having fingers or a dick up my arse, my own dick always reacted the same initially. My aim was to get him as hard as steel just before he blew. Just the thought of him painting his jizz across the two of us had me easing a third finger in.

He garbled a moan, eyes closing before springing back open when I nailed his prostate. "Yes, right there."

"You want me to keep going with my fingers?" I desperately hoped that wasn't the case, but I'd give him whatever he wanted.

My words had his half-open eyes snapping wide. "No. Cock." He reached out and grabbed me. I moaned, humour at his impatience bubbling to the surface.

Quickly freeing my fingers, I instructed, "Hold your legs."

Seb followed my instruction, his gaze now solely on my own.

I pressed against his opening, my breath catching

when just my head dipped inside. Tight and hot, just this was already fucking spectacular.

"More," Seb groaned.

A glance at his face told me he was okay, so I pushed deeper, pausing a moment before drawing out, then in, and then finally, I bottomed out.

Our moans were in unison, my own tapering off when I breathed through my need to start slamming into him. His legs wrapped around me, one hand now moving to his cock. His lips parting, eyes zeroing in on me, it was all too much, but still not enough.

"I'm good," he whispered, his lips curving.

I returned his smile as I pulled out before pushing back in, loving how he contracted around me, loving the steady flush of his skin.

I continued, hips angling and moving, pressing in and drawing out. My heart thudded in my ears along with my movements, the sound amplifying as I grew closer to losing my mind.

With increasingly erratic movements, I picked up speed. "Fuck." The word spilled out as Seb continued to jerk himself off, his own words rolling into one another incoherently.

A slight shift had the loudest groan spilling out of

his mouth. Wide-eyed, he focussed on me, his mouth forming an O. "There, holy fuck. There."

I arrowed in on the spot that I hoped like hell would push him over. With a surge forward, my legs shook, my toes straining against the mattress. "Fuck!" My release all but punched out of me, hard and fast. I shuddered, neck straining, and drove in twice more, a rush of contentment flooding through me when Seb went rigid and shot his load.

I sagged against him, aiming blindly for his mouth, somehow connecting and swiping my lips across his. Shifting my head to his neck, trying to catch my breath, I asked, "You good?"

A bob of his head followed, the quickness of his breaths matching my own. "Spectacular," he said with a chuckle.

I groaned at the movement, having no choice but to hold on to my junk and pull out carefully. "No laughing when you're clamped down on me," I grumbled lightly. Back on my knees, I stared down at the man before me.

"I bet I'm not looking quite so cute now, covered in cum," he challenged, eyes alive with humour.

I shook my head, amused. "You'll always be fucking cute, especially when covered in jizz." I pressed my lips to his for a brief kiss. "Let me go clean up. You want a shower or a cloth?"

"I could shower."

I nodded, wondering just how small his shower really was, and hoping like hell he exaggerated how unsuitable it was for two men.

***

HE WASN'T EXAGGERATING.

After a couple of near misses, and genuinely worrying for the both of us, I'd tapped out, much to Seb's humour, and stepped out of the shower.

I'd explained in no uncertain terms that in the future, my place needed to be the hub when he wanted his wicked way with me. His laughter had followed me out of the small bathroom.

Fortunately, he'd listened, and with another week passing us by and Seb being in my bed every night, it was easy for this to become my new norm.

Yeah, we worked together, but with him only being at Bar QK about twenty hours and us not working directly together, we weren't in each other's space all day. Though, I couldn't help but seek him out whenever just the memory of the touch and taste of him on my lips got the better of me.

In the bar, Marco—Lady Bra Ga when in drag—and I discussed the new music set he was interested in doing. While the set was his own and he didn't need my permission exactly, I appreciated him looping me in.

"I think the two will work well together," he said, explaining the swapping of two songs. "I just need to fine-tune the routine, and I'll need Adrian and Mo to join me on at least one of them."

I nodded in approval. "I agree. Are you able to organise rehearsal space? Or will the bar on Sunday morning do?" We didn't open till late every other Sunday, the only couple of days a month we didn't offer breakfast.

"We'll definitely need both, but I've got it sorted. The village hall near me is great at offering me their space."

I quirked my brow at that. "That's the one James is on the committee for, right?"

Marco quirked his brow back at me. "Maybe. I can't help it if he can't resist my charms."

My snort followed. "Charms, right, that's what we're calling it?"

"Hush," he said, giving me a nudge. A door opening drew Marco's attention away. "Ooh… and another gorgeous specimen…. How do you find such lickable staff?"

I flicked my gaze in the direction of the door, my eyes landing on Seb. My smile was instant.

"Alrighty then," Marco said, no doubt in response to my focussed attention, "this is the guy everyone's talking about. Got it."

Seb locked eyes on me, offered me a wink, and stepped over to Tom.

While I'd heard Marco's comment, I had no desire to know what people were saying. Plus, with my eyes following Seb's every movement, it was hard to concentrate.

Marco's sigh finally pulled me away, however.

"What?" I asked.

"Just you, finding this gorgeous beau," he said with exaggerated whimsy. "Obviously he's an amazing guy, since he adored my performance so much."

I laughed. "He did rave a little."

"Rave, right! I think I could make him my biggest fan."

Amused, I shook my head at Marco. "I thought that was James's job?"

A small shoulder lift preceded his words. "I'm not

sure I'm feeling it. He's all up for staying in at week-ends and cosying up at night."

The thought of me and Seb doing exactly that sounded like bliss. "And you don't want that?"

His nose scrunched up. "Maybe one day, but not yet and not with James."

"You need to sort that sooner rather than later. The guy's seriously into you."

A flash of guilt appeared on his face. "I know. Dumping someone sucks, especially when they're a good human being, you know?"

I bobbed my head, returning my gaze to Seb, smiling when he started laughing at something Tom said. A moment later, he turned and walked in my direction, his gaze flicking up to the window to the left of me and on the other side of the door. When his eyes widened, his mouth parting, I made to stand. My movement was cut off by the smash of glass. Instinctively, I covered my head, my heart pounding, and Seb's shout echoing in my head.

As the last large tin smashed to the ground, I was moving. "Seb," I called, standing before him. He'd crouched, covering his head with his arms. His frightened gaze shot to mine, and I reached out to him, hands shaking as I took in the few drops of blood on his face and the splashes of different coloured paint covering him.

I heard movement and swiftly looked in the direction of the noise, watching Marco dart outside. Fuck, if someone was still out there…. But then Tom rushed past me, and I refocused on Seb.

"You okay?" I led him towards the bar, away from the debris, and eased him back on a stool.

"I'm okay, I think," he said, wincing slightly as he touched one of the small cuts on his face. He then looked around the bar. "Is everyone else?"

I knew I should care, knew I should focus on others, but with Seb injured, no matter how insignificantly, I couldn't concentrate.

"I've called the police," Carla said, her voice taking me by surprise.

"Thanks." I glanced over at her. "Can you just check no one else was harmed?"

"Of course," she said, heading into the main bar from the open doorway.

My focus returned to Seb. "You can see okay, yeah? No glass went in your eyes or anything?"

"My eyes are fine. I'm okay." He huffed out a breath, then peered down at himself. A derogative snort escaped. "I suppose the different coloured paints are original. Almost supportive of the rainbow." While humour lit his voice, I heard the shake beneath it.

Unable to hold back, I reached out and curled my arms around him. Seb wrapped himself around me immediately as I hugged him in silence, offering the occasional kiss to the top of his head. The softness of his breathing was controlled as I imagined he was pulling himself together and getting on top of his emotions.

"I'm okay," he whispered after the quiet moment, and I eased back just as the sirens registered. "You go and speak to the police. I'll wait here."

"I've got him," Tom said, appearing at our side. His face was ashen, his voice low as his eyes connected with mine. Sorrow filled his gaze, my gut clenching for the guy. I got it. I did. This was too similar to the paint incident involving his brother. And while his brother was still in remand, there was the rest of his family he had to contend with.

"Thanks," I said before pressing a gentle kiss to Seb's lips. I angled a look over my shoulder, spotting the ambulance through the window. "Make sure you get looked over."

Seb nodded, and I stepped away, heading straight for Drake, relieved as hell he was one of the two cops who'd arrived.

It took over an hour for Drake and Linda, the officer on duty with him, to take statements and run through everything. The positive thing was Marco had spotted the make and model of the car that had peeled away just as he'd stepped outside—and the first three digits of the car's rego.

"I'm going to chase up with the other man involved in the incident involving Val and Seb," Drake said when we stood off to the side.

"That Rocky guy?" I asked.

"Yeah. The guy's out on bail, awaiting the news of his court date. He didn't get put on remand like Tom's brother. His record wasn't quite as grim." Drake sighed, looking tired. "You gave the video footage to Linda, yeah?"

I nodded, relieved we had cameras at the front of the building, a good reminder to add them to the blind spots that had hidden the graffiti incidents from a few weeks back. "Yeah."

"Good. We'll get it looked at, then will hopefully have enough to make an arrest."

"Whole lot of good that did last time," I said, the words falling out of my mouth. I winced, immediately saying, "Sorry. I know it was out of your hands."

Drake's jaw clenched as he bobbed his head. "I

get it. Just as pissed off as you are." His eyes then travelled to where I knew Seb was sitting. "He gonna be okay?"

I looked over at the man who'd become such an intrinsic part of my life. The paramedics had patched him up. No stitches were needed, and there were just a couple of shards they'd had to remove. "I'll make sure he is," I said. There was no doubt in my mind that Seb and I were a team. He'd have my back just as readily as I had his.

"That's good. I'll let you know as soon as I have news. Be sure to call your sister. I saw the press outside, so she'll be worried."

"Will do." I reached out and shook his hand.

After saying goodbye, I looked at the army of bodies in Bar QK, and despite the shattered glass, the fallen chairs and stools, and the red, blue, yellow, green, and purple paint that decorated so many surfaces, I managed a breath of relief.

The few tourist types had been allowed to leave, and since then, what was left was a handful of locals, the staff on duty, and two more who shouldn't be here. I expected they'd been called in by someone.

That was the thing. Bar QK was more than a simple place to come and grab a beer; we'd built a community. And with the familiar faces already in full-clean-up mode, working their arses off to not let a bunch of bigoted pricks get us down, a rush of emotion threatened to floor me.

"Hey." Seb's hand touched my forearm. "You doin' okay?"

I huffed out a laugh with a shake of my head. "Says the guy who's been injured." The twist in my stomach was visceral, painful when I looked at his wide eyes filled with concern.

"Hey," he said again, this time embracing me on his toes so his face could plant firmly at my neck. His voice was quiet, just for me. "I'm okay. This is not your fault, and there's nothing you could have done to prevent this."

His words were soft caresses across my skin, causing goosebumps to ripple across my arms. I sighed into the comfort he offered, not giving a shit that I was in the middle of my bar. I squeezed lightly, finally pulling away after he dotted a kiss to my neck.

Once settled back on his feet, he offered me a smile. "What do you need me to do?"

I shook my head. "You need to rest." There was no way I could let him carry on as though nothing had happened. Shock was a bastard of a thing and could easily creep up on him. And if that happened, I didn't want him to be in the middle of the room.

Seb pursed his lips before opening his mouth to speak. I cut him off by tugging him close and bending my knees slightly.

"I know you think you're fine, but I need you safe, and you need to decompress. Please," I added for good measure.

His gaze roamed mine, questions flickering in their depths. "Okay," he said finally. "Let me do something though. I need to."

There was no doubt he spoke the truth, and I expected the need was so he could busy his mind. "How about you head back to the office with Carla and see what she needs?"

He bobbed his head. "I can do that."

Relief slithered over me. I wanted him close by for sure, and out the back was the safest place for him. I grazed my lips across his, leaning into the kiss for a moment before edging back, eyes now on the room. I spotted Carla and called her over. "Will you head out back and arrange whatever needs to be sorted? Seb will help."

Her agreement was immediate. "'Course." She smiled at Seb, saying, "I'll deal with the insurance if you can sort a glazier," as they walked together, leaving for the office and giving me the time to properly take in all that had happened.

I had to believe that the CCTV had done its job and Drake would arrest the people who did this. With five eight-litre tins of paint that had smashed through the window, this was certainly not a one-person job. Not with the speed at which it had happened.

But knowing that the final incident to have stopped these shitheads for good—I hoped—had resulted in Seb's injuries and those of a couple of customers who'd been sliced by flying glass made me sick to my stomach.

Hate crimes. Just the thought of them sent my gut roiling. It was a fucking epidemic. The past three years, I'd been lucky to have run things relatively unscathed—lived my life focused on the bar and therefore in the bubble of protection it offered.

There was no way I'd let that bubble deflate. It had been sliced and battered, but hell if I'd not work my hardest to make sure me and mine were safe here. Screw the haters.

THE SMILE on my face threatened to split. It was at the point of hurting, but there was no way I was willing to pull back my happiness.

After four months of planning, it was finally showtime, and perfectly timed with the Sunshine Coast Pride Festival too.

A quick glance around showed a full house. The tables and chairs had been rearranged to allow for maximum capacity while still providing breathing room. And at a nice price per head for admission, it meant we had already raised several thousand for a Queensland based non-profit organisation.

After the nightmare a few months back, Elijah had charged out like some kind of warrior, determined to expand his own impact, as well as Bar

QK's, on the local LGBTIQ community. We'd all felt it that day, and the days that followed, but Elijah had put the media coverage to good use and made a stand.

And a few months later, with both of the bigoted idiots serving time—and another given community service and a caution—though admittedly not long enough as far as any of us were concerned, we were here, and the atmosphere was electric.

Lady Bra Ga was in her element, centre stage and performing so perfectly, the hairs on the back of my neck were standing on end.

"I don't think I'll ever get tired of watching her," I said to Tom as we stood at the end of the bar, both completely slayed by her performance.

"She's incredible," he said, his voice breathy.

I glanced over at him and smirked. "It's sweet that you have such a boner for her."

Even in the strobe lighting, I could tell he was blushing. Over the past few months, Tom had become a good friend. The whole shitshow of his family being turds had kicked up my desire to get to know him, as well as pulling him into the fold of the Bar QK family even deeper. "I'm not the only one. She's so hot."

I patted his arm, my sympathy genuine. Lady Bra

Ga had a confirmed reputation for being absolutely not interested in settling down, while Tom saw love hearts and absolutely wanted someone to call his. He'd admitted as much to me on several occasions… usually when the good vodka was flowing.

"Where's the boss man?" he asked, changing topics completely. The mention of Elijah had the same effect it always did. My heart tumbled over itself, the wings in my stomach taking flight at the possibility of seeing him.

I craned my neck, scanning the room, my gaze finally landing on him. "He's with Cole, just off the side of the stage." They were talking, heads tilted close together so they could hear, both sets of eyes roaming the bar.

When his wandering gaze settled on me, I felt the heat at the contact. Usually his eyes would widen, even just a little. Sometimes tongue would peek out to swipe at his bottom lip, and almost every time without fail, if he was close enough, he'd reach out to touch me in some way.

And despite the crowd separating us, despite the shadows and the flashing lights, it was as if I could feel his touch across the distance.

"You guys are impossible," Tom grumbled, but there was no bite in his tone.

"Uh-huh." I knew it, so did Elijah, and I wouldn't want it any other way.

"When's the official moving in day?" he asked.

"Two weeks on Sunday." I grinned at the memory of how Elijah had asked, how his tender words combined with him giving me head had meant I hadn't needed any convincing to say yes. I'd already started moving lots of my things over, which wasn't a hardship since I spent 90 percent of my time there.

I angled back to Tom, and he bobbed his head. "That's great, save him from grouching when he's working that you're not at his place waiting for him." He threw me a grin with his words.

"Ha! Not sure anything will stop his grouchy ways."

"Whose grouchy ways?"

Elijah's heat registered in time with his words, followed immediately by his hand on my waist. With his presence came the calm I associated with the man who had my heart. It was at complete odds with the impact his heated looks gave, but just as comforting.

I quirked my brow at him, leaning into his touch. "You really need for me to point out the grouchy one?"

My words resulted in a pinch of my arse. I laughed. "Hands off the goods."

He angled towards me, his breath brushing against my cheek, then neck before he said, "I thought your arse was mine?"

I grinned and he eased back. "True."

"And no take-backs," he said with a smirk. "Taking back gifts is all levels of tacky."

"You're ridiculous," I said, my snort somehow hurting my throat when it came out loud and hard.

"And you're cute," he challenged.

My eye-roll was immediate, as was Tom's "And I'm out!"

Elijah took his place next to me at the bar. "You having a good night?"

I nodded, flicking my gaze to the stage and the dancers as Lady Bra Ga prepared for her next set. "The best." I forced conviction into my voice when I said, "What you've done here tonight is amazing."

"And long overdue."

I shook my head at him in frustration, hating that he continued to beat himself up. "Let's stay in the moment while still looking forward, yeah? Tonight is great, and what you have in the works is even better."

"It's exciting, right?" Finally, a look of satisfaction crossed over his features.

"It is, and I'm proud as hell." There were a couple of local non-profits we'd been in contact with, looking at events and activities outside of the annual celebrations, including a surfing one that I was psyched about.

Softness settled in his gaze as he zeroed in on me. "Thank you. I think we can actually make a difference."

Rising onto my tiptoes, I angled up so I could be close to his mouth. "Together, we really can," I said breathily before pressing against him, my mouth capturing his. There was little doubt in my mind that as a couple we'd hold strong, and as a community, we'd continue to work our arses off to help make our home a better place.

HAVE YOU CAUGHT UP WITH MY TRUE-BLUE SERIES? It's now complete with book five, *It's Not You*, which is a stand-alone read in my sexy, low-angst romance series!

I hope Seb and Elijah made you happy sigh. If you're looking for more Aussie romances, check out

Thicker Than Water, which features a smart-mouthed and delicious wolf shifter. If paranormal isn't your thing, check out **Amalgamated** where you can visit the Australian outback.

Don't forget about my True-Blue series, starting with *Let Me Show You*. Plus, *Always For You*, a stand-alone short in the series, is available for free download to my newsletter subscribers.

Diverse Voices: http://diversevoices.org.au/

Diverse Voices is a non-profit organisation that largely relies on fundraising to cover their costs. Please take a moment to check out their sponsor a call campaign.

Sunshine Coast Pride: https://www.sunshinecoast-pride.org/

Sunshine Coast Pride is designed to help the gay community in the area network, support and band together in mutual celebration, recognition and strength.

Becca Seymour lives and breathes all things book related. Usually with at least three books being read and two WiPs being written at the same time, life is merrily hectic. She tends to do nothing by halves, so happily seeks the craziness and busyness life offers.

Living on her small property in Queensland with her human family as well as her animal family of cows, chooks, and dogs, Becca appreciates the beauty of the world around her and is a believer that love truly is love.

To check for updates head to Becca's website:
https://beccaseymour.com
You can sign up for her newsletter here:
https://landing.mailerlite.com/webforms/
landing/r9f0i4
Plus, join her Facebook group, which she shares
with the awesome Louisa Masters here:
https://www.facebook.com/
groups/seymourbookswithmasterfulmen/

facebook.com/beccaseymourauthor
twitter.com/beccaseymour_
instagram.com/authorbeccaseymour
bookbub.com/authors/becca-seymour